Bob Moats

I0567281

Doyle's Justice

By Bob Moats

Doyle's Justice

This book is licensed for your personal use only. This book may not be re-sold or given away to other people. If you would like to share this book with another person, please purchase an additional copy for each recipient. If you're reading this book and did not purchase it, or it was not purchased for your use only, please purchase your own copy. Thank you for respecting the hard work of this author.

This is a work of pure fiction. Names, characters, places, and incidents either are the product of the author's imagination or are used fictitiously, and any resemblance to actual persons, living or dead, business establishments, events, or locales is entirely coincidental.

ISBN – 978-0-9960634-7-0

For information and address:
Magic 1 Productions
P.O. Box 524, Fraser MI 48026-0524
Website: http://murdernovels.com
Cover design by Bob Moats

Extra special thanks to:

Special thanks to Val Brooks who edited this book and for all her great suggestions.

Thanks to the pre-beta readers Cindy Gross Valstad, Susan Haughton, and Al Norris.

Thank you for purchasing this book. I hope you enjoy it as much as I enjoyed writing it for my faithful readers. If you liked the book please feel free to write an honest review on the product page where you got this book from. I'd appreciate it. Please feel free to email me to tell me what you thought about my stories. I love hearing from the readers. I can be reached at murdernovels@bobmoats.com thanks again!

Doyle's Justice

Chapter 1

Creeping quietly through the woods was made difficult due to the dead leaves of autumn covering the mossy ground. Every step resulted in a muted crackling sound that disturbed the silence of the late night three o'clock journey. The man dressed in black, to help hide his appearance, crept up behind the small log building to drop off the surprise for his old nemesis. His stealthy walk in the woods was being made more difficult by the body he was dragging. Even wrapped up in the plastic sheeting, the package was difficult to pull over the morning dew on the colorful rug of leaves.

The dark figure didn't care if it was hard to maneuver through the woods. He had a goal, a mission to deliver his gift. He finally broke through the stand of trees and into the small backyard of the building sitting empty in the moonlight. He knew the occupant was away, but his present would be there

4

upon the resident's return. Removing the plastic sheeting, he set the body against the small wood pump house that provided well water for the cabin. He turned the body to face the building and was delighted by the cleverness of his gift. A present to the one person he had a desire to involve in his murders - Arthur Doyle.

~~*~~

Doyle woke feeling a chill even though the temperature in his apartment was set at a steady seventy-eight degrees. He moved closer to the woman in bed with him for the body heat. She turned softly to meet his body and then put her arm over him, though she was still asleep. Instinct took over when one felt a closeness to another person. If she wasn't now used to the man in bed with her, she probably would have lashed out at Doyle. He knew to always be ready for an attack from his sleeping beauty.

Doyle lifted his head to look over the woman to see what time it was by the clock on the bedside stand. Three-thirty - it was going to be hard to get back to sleep. Doyle was a light sleeper, a seemingly unbreakable habit from his former FBI training - be alert for any situation or attack by the enemy. He put his head back down and looked at Val, his sometimes live-in girlfriend, barely seeing her in the dim light of the outer room.

His mind went back to the day he met her in the pool hall while he was searching for a bookie. Not that he needed a bookie, but the creep was part of a missing persons assignment Doyle had. Val was a waitress at the pool hall and they expressed a desire for each other. He had just broken up with another woman and he wondered if Val was only a rebound affair. She made him happy in many ways, mostly sexual, but she was intelligent and had a great sense of humor, too. She needed a sense of humor to be with Doyle.

He did fall back to sleep, totally unaware of what was happening fifty-two miles away at his cabin by Lake Metamora.

The next morning, he heard Val doing something in his kitchen. Probably making breakfast, which he didn't eat. He got up and dressed to go to the office at his private investigating business. Val had her own key to his apartment and would let herself out.

"Good morning," she said as he came out to her.

"Keep your good mornings to yourself," he grinned. "I didn't sleep very well, and if it weren't for going out to solve crimes, I'd stay in bed," he said, and kissed her lightly on the cheek.

She grabbed his shirt, pulled him back to her and planted a big kiss on his lips. "That's better," she said with a smile. He went to get his Sig Sauer 9 handgun and put it in the quick release holster under his left arm. He slid the new .38 in the holster behind him and looked in the mirror by the front door.

"I get older looking every day. I hate it," he said.

6

"You could stand to darken the grey in your hair. For a man of fifty-one, you're getting grey early."

"It makes me look wise and distinguished."

"It makes you look extinguished," she said with a subtle laugh.

"Whatever, I have to go to work. I'll talk to you later." He grabbed his jacket to cover his weapons and left the apartment. As he drove across the city of Detroit to his office, he thought about the affairs that brought him to his present state. He accidently shot the mayor of Detroit during a hostage exchange. Not a deadly shot, but it gave the mayor a nice scar on the side of his head so he'd always remember Doyle. He quit the Detroit police as a homicide detective after that. The job was getting to him and the incident with the mayor's outburst over being wounded was the final straw.

Doyle pulled up to the back of his building and went in the back door. He entered and found his partner, Oscar, talking to Marge, their secretary and receptionist.

"Hey Art, Marge and I were talking about ways to bring in more clients."

"More clients? If we get any more than we're getting now, I'll have to hire a couple ex-cops to help out. Since the advertising I've been doing, we've been doing nicely in the client department."

"True, but we need to keep up."

"What do you have going?" Doyle asked.

"Nothing glamorous, just following a cheating wife. Husband came in this morning and hired us."

"Well, it's a case. Surveillance is an art form," Doyle said.

"It is when you don't have to do it. I have to go follow the woman when she leaves for her yoga class this afternoon. I think she's probably bending her body for the instructor."

Marge laughed and said, "Since you opened for business last month, I'm getting to like this job. I've met some very interesting people."

"You evidently didn't get out much before," Doyle said.

"Actually, I didn't. I was too much of a housewife. While my late husband was out chasing criminals around Detroit, I was baking pies."

"Maybe someday you could bake us a nice apple pie?" Oscar asked.

"You think too much about food, Oscar," Doyle said.

"Hey, I'm a growing boy," Oscar replied.

"Growing around the middle, yes. You need to keep in shape for any foot chases."

"Easier to shoot them than to run," Oscar said with grin.

"Do you realize all the interrogations and paperwork you have to go through when you fire your weapon and you're no longer a cop? I spent three days going over all that from the shootings I did over the Kellogg case. I'm using my wits and my fists from now on."

"Well, whatever, I have to go follow a wife. I hope she's good-looking, at least. Talk later." Oscar picked up a small briefcase and went out.

"How are you feeling this morning, Arthur?" Marge asked.

"A little tired, didn't sleep well this morning. I felt a little uneasy and it was difficult to stay asleep."

"Something bothering you?"

"I don't know. It's just a feeling I have that something is wrong," Doyle said.

"Maybe you're developing a woman's intuition. I get those feelings, too, when something bad is going to happen."

"I won't mind the intuition, as long as I don't have other women's problems. I'm usually crabby, but not just once a month," he said, grinning.

"I'm too old now for that curse. At sixty-seven, arthritis is my curse."

The phone rang on Marge's desk, she answered. "Doyle Investigations, may I help you?" She listened and then said, "Please wait." She put the phone on hold and said to Doyle, "You have a call from a Sheriff Twain out in Metamora. Isn't that where your cabin is?"

"Yes it is. Thanks, I'll take it at my desk." He went around the new partition walls he had installed, sat at his desk, and wondered why Mike Twain was calling him. He grew up with Mike in Oxford and they both went into law enforcement. Mike went to the county sheriff's department and Doyle went to the FBI, then to the Detroit police. He sat at his desk and hit the button on the phone.

"Mike, what's up?" he asked.

"Art, got a problem. How soon do you think you can get up here?" the voice said in his ear.

"Well, it takes an hour to drive, why?"

"We got an anonymous call this morning that there was a body out back of your cabin. I'd like you to come and identify the body. We have no idea who she is."

Doyle knew that Gwen, his last girlfriend, was now in Cleveland, so it couldn't be her. "I can come right up, but give me some time to get organized."

"No problem. It's cold enough to keep the body presentable. We'll wait until you get here. You may see something we don't."

"I'll be there shortly. Thanks for the call, Mike." He hung up and stood and said over the wall, "Marge, I have to go to my cabin. It seems they found a dead woman in my back yard."

"Oh dear, could that be what you were feeling uneasy about this morning?"

Doyle thought about that, "Yeah, it could be. I'll be back when I can. Tell Oscar where I am and to keep an eye on the business."

"I will," she said as Doyle went out back to his car. He drove over to I-75 and headed up to his cabin.

He said to himself as he drove, "I hope it's no one I know."

*

Chapter 2

Doyle saw the sheriff's car and a big black van parked on his property when he arrived. He had never met the coroner, since he never had to deal with death in this town. Plus, he wasn't around that much to meet very many officials, other than his friend Mike. He parked on the grass since the county vehicles took over the drive. He got out and walked around to the back of his cabin.

"Art, sorry to bring you up here, I'm sure you are busy enough in the big city," his friend said.

"Crime is a little slow today. Now, what's the deal?"

The sheriff led him to the body of a woman positioned so she was sitting propped up against the small pump house, her empty eyes looking towards the cabin. Doyle leaned down to study the face of the woman. "She looks familiar. I think I knew her when she was younger. Tammy Gilpin. She was a girl who had a crush on me, I'm pretty sure it's her." The girl's face was giving way to being ravaged by decomposition. "There was no ID around her body?"

Mike went to Doyle and handed him an index card in a plastic evidence bag. Doyle read it through the plastic. It was typed, "*Hey Doyle, she didn't need that treatment you gave her. Now her death is on your hands.*"

Doyle stood, looked at his friend and said, "I didn't treat her badly. I may have ignored her, she wasn't in my circle of friends. At least I didn't think so. She hardly ever talked to me."

"How did you know she had a crush on you?"

"She made a card one Valentine's Day and slipped it to me, before running away. It was a heart saying she had a crush on me, that's how I knew. She never came around me after that. I didn't know what to do. She wasn't beautiful, she was plain, but nice. Besides, I had a girlfriend, Gloria Waschevski. Tammy knew that."

"Well, someone thinks you gave her the bum's rush. Whoever did this, has targeted you personally."

"I'm not happy about this. I never meant to hurt this girl, and I sure didn't murder her. I hope this killer isn't going to take out all the women I rejected in my youth. We'd have bodies all over my backyard," he said, with a grim expression.

"A lovelorn serial killer. Now that would be one for the books. Did this girl have any family? I don't remember her very well."

"She stayed in the background most of the time. You were too hung up on Cindy Van Pak to pay any attention to other women. Whatever happened to her?"

"I married her. I guess we haven't talked much since you moved away."

"Well, we'll have to do some catching up. As I recall, Tammy's mother lived in a small house south of Oakwood Road on Lapeer Road in Oxford. It was on the side of the road going north. She was brought up here from Oxford just to be dumped in my backyard." Doyle shook his head.

"I'll have one of my deputies look up the mother and see if she's still there."

"Let me know. I'd like to go give my condolences." Doyle moved away from the body as two men moved in to pick it up and place it on a gurney.

"Art, this is Elwood Dowes, our county coroner," Mike introduced the man as he came up.

"I hear you're from the city. You were a cop?"

"For far too long, yes."

"I read in the Detroit News about you shooting the mayor."

"I'll be glad when that dies out. I'm not proud of my shot, but I did save the ingrate's life."

"I understand, hard to shoot one head when another is moving."

"Exactly, I like you Elwood," Doyle said with a smile.

"Pleasure to meet you, Doyle. I never cared for that mayor much. Excuse me, I have to find out how this poor woman was murdered."

"Let me know, Elwood," Doyle requested.

The coroner went to help the two assistants bag the woman and take her to the van.

"Could this be a jilted male who had a crush on the vic and wants to lash out at you?" Mike asked.

"Damned if I know. Hopefully this will be the only one," Doyle replied.

"Are you going back to the city?"

"Nah, I may stay around until Elwood gets some results. I want to do some investigating, if it's all right with you?"

"Hell, you can take over, we're busy enough with all the tourists coming to ogle the fall colors. Damn people traipsing all over the county getting in all kinds of trouble. That's the problem with being so close to a state campground. All the weekend warriors think they can go anywhere they want. My deputies are spread thin. No, have at it, and hopefully you'll get to the heart of the matter."

"Since it involved my property and a girl I once knew, I think I'd like to solve this. I'll keep you informed. Just how did they bring her back here? There's only two ways, by boat or from Baldwin Road."

"Whoever dragged her here came through the woods, probably from Baldwin. I had forensics look it over before you got here and they found really nothing, other than drag marks. They did say she was wrapped in a plastic bag or something. There was no dirt or leaves on her body. If she was dragged, she would have been dirty. The team is looking around Baldwin now to see if they can get any tire tracks."

"Well, let me know what they find," Doyle said, then asked, "Feel like coming in to warm up?"

"I thought you'd never ask. I've always wanted to see inside this cabin."

Doyle led his friend into the cabin. It had been closed up for a month so it was a bit musty. Doyle kicked on the heater and it was warm shortly thereafter. They sat at the kitchen table and talked about their lives since they last saw each other.

"You got a wife or girlfriend?" Mike asked.

"Part-time girlfriend. She's great, but I'm not ready to settle down, and she knows it. I can't say where it will go, but I'm having a good time getting there. I was married for three years, then my wife was killed two years ago in a car accident. Drunk driver ran a red light and t-boned her car. The paramedics said she went fast. Thankfully. Since then I haven't had the desire to get that involved again."

"Tough, I was never without Cindy. We've been married for almost thirty years. Damn, time goes fast," Mike said, then went silent.

"Are you still happy with her?"

"Yes, I am. She's a wonderful woman, and I was lucky to find her."

"Maybe if I'm still around for a few days, we can get together."

"That works for me," Mike said, just as his radio beeped. "Excuse me," he said, then answered on the microphone attached to his jacket. He was being called back in, they were short of officers. He agreed and signed off. "Damn, can't get a minute's rest." Mike handed Doyle a card with his cell phone number and said, "Call me later if you'll be around." They stood, and Doyle followed Mike to the door and they went out.

"Talk later," Mike said and went to his car. Doyle watched his friend drive away and went back around the building to the pump house. He walked around the structure studying the ground. It had been walked over by the forensic people, the coroner and the police. But he could see the drag marks in the dirt. He followed them into the woods and could see where they were going. He followed them through the woods until he came out to the road. He was standing by the place where a car might have parked to drop off the body. He could see where forensics must have made a cast of one tire and hoped they were equipped to track the tread. If not, he would see if Oscar could send it to his friends in the forensic department at the precinct. One day, Captain Cadeem would be gone and Doyle could go back to his old precinct again without worrying about running into the jerk.

Doyle looked around the area. It was mostly woods and not much else. He turned back to his cabin and when he got to the door he found it was partially open. He drew his Sig and carefully pushed the door open further. He heard a noise and rushed in with his gun out front. He yelled, "Freeze," but the only thing in the cabin was a raccoon. He laughed out loud as the animal scurried out the door.

"I have to remember to close the door all the way," he said to himself. He went back outside and sat on the wooden lawn chair, watching the raccoon sitting on his lawn watching Doyle. He got up and went back in the cabin, and when he came out again, he had a couple pieces of stale bread. He sat down and tore the bread into small pieces, throwing them out to the animal. The raccoon scrambled to the bread and gathered as much as it could, then ran off.

Doyle thought he shouldn't tempt the animal into getting treats from him. But he loved to watch the animals around his cabin. There were occasional deer walking through, and luckily, no bigger animals than that. He had heard there may be bear and wildcats or cougars, but never saw any. He wasn't ready to face a bear in his cabin. He just liked watching them from a distance.

Doyle wasn't aware, but he was being watched from nearby along the shore. The person was hidden in the bushes and said to himself, "You relax now, Doyle, I'll keep you busy enough."

*

Chapter 3

Doyle's cell phone rang out its *Jaws* theme and he looked at the caller ID, it was Oscar.

"I debated whether I wanted to answer or not, but I wanted to be sure the office hadn't burned down," Doyle said when he answered.

Oscar's voice came out from the phone, "Nope, no luck. What's going on? Marge said they found a body at your cabin."

"Behind the cabin, and it was a woman I sort of knew years ago."

"You need me to help?"

"Not right now. I'll call you if it gets to that point. Otherwise, take care of the business and the clients."

"Sure, I work while you sit around your cabin enjoying life," Oscar said.

"Sounds good to me, I'll be back in a day or two, depending on how my investigation goes. The coroner is going to let me know exactly how she died. I may need you to do a trace on a tire print, if they can't handle it here."

"Another visit to forensics. Maybe I'll visit Cadeem and give him your best wishes."

"Yeah, tell him to drop dead. Don't even mention we're playing P.I. or he may see what kind of trouble to get us in. I don't trust the man."

"I'll just stay away then."

"Are you in the office?" Doyle asked.

"Yep, watching Marge knitting me a scarf. I asked for bright red. What color do you want?"

"Whatever, black I guess."

"I'll tell her. You think you may be up there for a few days?"

"I'm figuring on it. There was a note on the body blaming me for her death. I don't like that. So, I'm going to hang in until I find something."

"Okay, call if you need me."

"I will," Doyle said and they finished.

Doyle relaxed on the chair a while longer, admiring the lake. He was getting hungry so he stood and closed up the cabin. He went to his car and drove down to Oxford to a restaurant. He had a meal and then decided to see if Tammy's mother still lived in the house on Lapeer. He knew where it was, so he drove there.

The house looked run down, hadn't been painted or fixed up in years, he figured. There was an old Buick in the drive. It had to be from around the fifties and it looked just as bad as the house. As he pulled into the driveway, he looked at the mail box and the name on it read 'Gilpin.' Maybe they were still there.

He pulled closer to the house and parked. He saw curtains move a little as he got out, so someone was home. He went to the concrete block porch that looked like it was built in pieces. The blocks wobbled a bit as he stepped up. He hoped the back was less hazardous. The door suddenly flew open.

An old woman with wild grey hair shooting out from her head and lots of deep wrinkles stood there in the doorway. "I know you. You were that snotty little kid, Arthur Doyle. My daughter did nothing but talk about you when she was a kid. I got sick of hearing about you. You ignored her, and broke her heart."

"Ma'am, I barely knew your daughter. She wasn't even one of my friends. I'm sorry if she was hurt, but I never led her on."

The old woman was silent. "My daughter was a little backwards in the head. She imagined things a lot. I suppose she imagined that you scorned her. Sorry."

"No problem. Has a sheriff come by to talk to you?" Doyle hated to ask, but he wanted to know where she was in this situation.

"Yeah, I know all about Tammy's murder. She probably brought it on herself, all that flirting she did with strange men."

"Mrs. Gilpin, I don't think this was a stranger who killed her. May I come in to talk?"

19

She stood staring at Doyle, then she looked back into her house. Finally she said, "Okay, excuse the mess."

"I'm not worried about your house. I just need to talk about Tammy."

The woman opened the door and Doyle went in. The living room was just off the front door, and it was a mess. There were boxes and trash piled up everywhere. Not foul trash, but junk that most people would throw out. He figured she was a hoarder. She invited him into the dining room, which was a little cleaner. There was a small dining table and three chairs. She pointed to one and asked him to sit. He pulled the chair out and was startled by a cat hissing at him.

"Damn, Hairy, stop that," she yelled at the cat and pushed him off the chair. "I call him Hairy because he has so much hair."

Doyle smiled and wanted to tell her that cats have fur, not hair. But it wouldn't do much good to start calling the cat Furry, so he let it go. He sat on the chair even though there was an abundance of fur on the seat. He'd have to brush good when he got back to the cabin. He sat and looked behind the woman as she sat. He saw two more cats on a shelf unit, both staring at him. He could face down criminals, but the cats staring at him was unnerving.

"So, you never had a thing for my daughter?" she began.

"Uh, no. I knew of her, but she wasn't one of my friends. She was much younger than I was."

"Like I said, she had imaginary loves. Crazy girl, I should have had her tested when she was younger. You said this murder may have been done by someone she knew and not a stranger?"

"It's looking that way." He paused, then said, "Mrs. Gilpin, I'm a private investigator now, I just left the Detroit Police after a lot of years. I'm going to investigate to see if I can find out who killed your daughter. What can you tell me about anyone she associated with?"

"She was a wild child, she was always with some bum. They would just use her and then drop her when she got clingy. She would bring them in the back door to her room and they'd be in there for way too long. She was a slut."

That surprised Doyle, he remembered her as a quiet, shy girl. But people change over the years. "When was the last time you saw her?" he asked.

"Yesterday morning. She said she was going to town to buy some women things. It was around nine in the morning."

"She was alone?"

"Yes, she didn't bring anyone home with her. That surprised me. That was the last time I saw her."

"I hate to say this, but you don't seem too upset over her death."

"I'm not. She was a pain in the ass. Always in the way and complaining about my stuff. It's my stuff, why should she worry. Well, she's gone now and I can put more stuff in her room."

Doyle was thinking like mother, like daughter. Both a bit off center. "Where would she have gone shopping?"

"That big store off Lapeer, in the city. I've never been in there, they're too expensive."

"Where did Tammy get her money from?"

"She'd hit up the men she saw, they would take care of her. I think she was charging for sex. Slut."

Doyle was starting to get a picture of this family, so he wanted to get out. The place was starting to smell of cat box and he saw two more cats on the kitchen counter through the door. He stood and thanked her. She followed him to the front door, then he paused. "When you first saw me, you knew who I was. It's been years, and I've never met you before. How'd you know it was me?"

"Tammy had pictures of you from back then, and she had one picture of you from last month. It was from out of the newspaper, you shot the mayor of Detroit, it said."

Now Doyle was becoming a celebrity even among the poor people miles from Detroit. "Thanks for that. If I find out who did this, I'll stop by and let you know." He stepped carefully onto the porch and went to his car. He looked back and saw four cats in the front window staring at him. The creeps crawled back into his spine and he moved quickly to get away.

He stopped at the sheriff's office and asked for his friend Mike. They directed him to where Mike was set up at his desk. Doyle came up behind him and tickled his ear. Mike shot up and took a swing at the unknown assailant. Doyle ducked and came up laughing.

"You're a nervous person. If I knew it would bother you so much, I wouldn't have done it."

"Oh, yes you would have. You always were a mean kid growing up. Not mean rotten, just annoyingly mean. What are you doing here?"

"I talked to Tammy's mother. She's a real winner," Doyle said.

"From what I've heard, the woman had a rough life. Parents abused her, husband was a bastard and abused her. Tammy was a little hellion and verbally abused her. I'm surprised the woman didn't shoot up a mall," Mike said.

"That is sad. I didn't get her whole story. I have to stop judging people by first sight. Anything from the coroner about Tammy's death?"

"Yeah, she was strangled. Elwood said it looked like a wire around the throat. She died quickly."

*

Chapter 4

Doyle wasn't fond of strangulation. A bullet or a knife was quicker, but losing your breath was something that bothered Doyle. He frequently had problems breathing during his sleep. He worried he would stop breathing one night. So, it bothered him to think of Tammy having the breath taken from her.

"So it was murder, then?"

"Unless she strangled herself, yes," Mike said, with a laugh.

"Do you think Tammy's mother could have strangled her? She seemed to be pretty strong."

"It's possible," he replied. "I know she caused problems last year in a party store and it took three of my officers to get her into the patrol car."

"That note could have referred to her being mad at me. Taking her daughter for granted. When I visited her, she expressed that feeling. I felt bad about it, but I didn't do anything wrong except to not acknowledge Tammy's affections."

"As you said before, you didn't acknowledge a lot of women's affections. I'm sure they all wouldn't hold a grudge against you. At least not enough to murder for it."

"Affairs of the heart can suddenly go really wrong. I've seen it as a cop in Detroit. Lover's quarrels and jilted boyfriends stalking and murdering their exes. People get really crazy when they think they're in love."

"I'm glad we don't have that much craziness out here in the sticks," Mike said.

"This area is just as prone to crazies as in Detroit. It's everywhere."

"Yeah, I guess so. It's just that we don't have as many people who could be crazy as you do." He grinned and stood. "Want some coffee?"

"No, thanks. Don't touch it."

"Well, we have a little coffee cream left you can drink," Mike said with a chuckle.

"Can't this place afford soda pop?"

"Now that you mention it, we may have a can or two hidden away for all you sissy boys who don't drink coffee. I'll see what we have." He went off while Doyle waited. He looked around the room, it was a typical cop shop - desks, file cabinets and lots of paper. There were two deputies in the room, one doing paperwork, the other talking to a woman at his desk. She looked upset, probably a lover's spat. What a nutty world, Doyle thought.

Mike came back with a Vernor's Ginger Ale in a can for Doyle. He handed it to him. Doyle studied the can and said, "How long have you had this here? I haven't seen this style of can in years and I used to drink Vernor's a lot."

"Occasionally, we confiscate goods from a car, it probably was in there and got lost in storage," Mike smirked.

Doyle popped the top and took a sip. "Well, it tastes all right. Now, have your forensic people run that tire tread yet?"

"They're working on it, last I heard. It was a wide tread, probably from a big SUV or truck. They don't have an exact tire model match yet, but they will."

"If they don't come up with a match, let me send it to my partner and he can have our forensic people run it," Doyle offered.

"Must be nice to have all that expensive equipment at your disposal," Mike said. "I talked to Cindy and she remembers you. If you're around this weekend, we can get together and reminisce."

"Sounds good to me. I'm going to go explore a couple places where Tammy may have hung out and see if anyone saw her with anyone. Her mother said she picked up a number of men and brought them home."

"There probably are a few bars she could have hung out at to troll for men."

"My thoughts, too. Do you have a photo of her that I can show?" Doyle asked.

Mike reached over his desk to a pile of folders and took the top one. He opened it and removed a photo, then went to a copier in a corner of the room. He ran off a couple copies and handed one to Doyle.

Doyle looked at it and winced, it wasn't the nicest picture. "Well, this should make a few people squeamish. Thanks, I'll call if I get anything."

"Or, stop back for more Vernor's, there was a six pack in the fridge." He laughed.

Doyle smiled and said he would. "Talk later," he said as he left the room.

He went back out to his car and stood looking around the area. He grew up in this town and it hadn't changed much. He got in his car and drove to a bar he knew well. It was the place where he had his first beer back when he could fake his age.

He pulled into the lot and saw the building hadn't changed in years. It was a plain front with an overhang above the door. The sign was the same, "Glory Hole Bar" and he never understood the reference. He figured it was some sexual innuendo. He exited his car and went to the door.

Bob Moats

Inside, he found it had been redecorated in a more modern style. The tables and chairs were new and the bar had been given a facelift. There was one man behind the bar and he looked familiar to Doyle. Then he realized it was someone from his past, Darryl Epstein. He wasn't close friends with the man, but they had an occasional cause to talk.

Doyle went to sit at the bar as the man was washing glasses. He looked up and said he'd be there shortly. Doyle looked around the room, other than the new furniture and a new juke box, it really hadn't changed much. Like a woman getting older, more make-up that can't hide the ravages of time.

The bartender came over to Doyle, wiping his hands on a towel. He started to ask what Doyle wanted to drink, when he stopped. "Hey, I know you. You're Art Doyle, right?"

"You got me, Darryl. How's things for you?"

"Not bad. After you moved away, I got an inheritance from my dad, enough money to buy this bar. I cleaned it up a little, but it's the same old story. Lots of drunks and loose women. Not much really changed. I heard you went into the FBI?"

"Yep, ten years before I got out. Then I joined the Detroit Police and worked my way up to homicide detective."

"Wow, homicide in Detroit? That must have kept you busy. Still with the DPD?"

"No, as a matter of fact, I'm a private investigator now. I have my office in Detroit, and we've been fairly busy."

"A P.I. and in the big city. I always figured you would become a cop or a criminal," he said with a laugh. "Whatcha drinking?"

Doyle smiled and said, "Got any Vernors?"

"I sure do, it's fairly popular around here. Too bad the bottling company was finally sold to Dr. Pepper in Texas. It's never been the same as when it was bottled in Detroit."

Darryl pulled a can from his fridge and gave it and a glass to Doyle. The can was different than the one Mike gave him. Maybe that one was an original. He'd have to get it back from Mike to put in his office.

"What brings you here, Art?"

"I don't know if you heard that Tammy Gilpin was murdered?"

"Wow, no, I hadn't heard. No one has been in today yet. When?"

"The sheriffs got a call about a body behind a cabin I own up on Lake Metamora. I came up from the city and identified the woman as Tammy. It looks like she was murdered last night and dumped early this morning."

"Now who would want to kill old Tammy? But, then again, she was picking up a good number of men here in the bar. I don't know where they went to, but they would go out together. I felt sorry for her, she seemed to be a wretched soul."

"Was she in here last night?" Doyle asked.

"Couldn't tell you. I was off last night. I can ask Amber when she comes in. She worked last night."

Doyle handed Darryl his card and said, "Call me if Amber saw her, and who she may have been with."

"You don't think one of my customers could have killed her?"

"Can't say, but it could have been someone who knew Tammy and followed her. She may not have even met up with her killer here. Tammy's mother said she saw her last, yesterday. She was going to some store." Doyle drank down the Vernor's, feeling gaseous from the intense carbonation.

Doyle stood, "If you find out that Tammy was here last night, call me. Thanks Darryl, good to see you again."

They said their goodbyes and Doyle went out to his car. The wind was getting even chillier for September. He had an extra winter-type jacket in the back seat in case. He reached back and put it on over his sport coat. He got in the car and drove out figuring on hitting the one big store on Lapeer Road. He wasn't familiar with it, since it was built after he moved away. He wasn't even sure what it was.

He drove down Lapeer until he saw a big building with a sign saying 'Value Time Stores.' He figured it might be the place and pulled in. He went into the store and asked for the manager. A woman came up and asked if she could help him.

"I hope so. Do you know a Tammy Gilpin?"

"Yes, I do. She works here."

*

Chapter 5

That statement really threw Doyle. Tammy's mother never said she was working. When he asked her where Tammy was getting her money, the mother said from men.

"Okay, when was she last here?" Doyle asked.

"And who are you?" the woman asked back.

"I'm sorry, I was just surprised by your answer. I'm a private investigator and I'm investigating Tammy's murder."

Now that shook up the woman. "What? Tammy's dead? When?"

"Sometime late last night. Can we go somewhere less public to talk?"

"Of course, follow me," she said and turned. Doyle followed her to a door going into the back of the store. She led him to her office, then she asked him to sit.

"Thanks. You said Tammy worked here. How many days a week?"

"About three days a week. We don't let employees work more than 32 hours a week or we will have to pay for their health insurance."

"Sure, don't help out people so they can have good health."

"That's unfair, Mr. ..."

"Doyle, Art Doyle. So, Tammy worked part-time here. Was she working last night?"

"No, she was off. What happened to her?"

"She was murdered, that's all I can say right now. What's your name?"

"I'm Sally Harden, store manager," she answered.

"Okay Sally, how long has she worked here?"

"About a year. She was a good employee. It's going to be hard to replace her."

"What were her hours, usually?"

"She worked mostly days, she wanted her nights free."

"Did you know what she did at night?"

"I knew she was somewhat of a party girl. She told me about a few of the men she met at the bars."

"Anyone in particular that may have had a reason to kill her?" Doyle asked.

"None that I can think of. She just mentioned them briefly, she didn't go into details about them."

"Would any of your other employees know who she may have been hanging with?"

"They might. There are a few in the break room if you'd like to talk to them?" she offered.

"Yes, that would be good, if you don't mind?"

"No, if it helps find the person who killed Tammy, it's fine with me. If you could come with me, I'll take you there." She stood and Doyle followed her out of the office. They went to another door in the back and there were about five people sitting at tables eating bag lunches.

She called to everyone's attention, "I need your undivided attention for a moment. This gentleman has to ask a few questions, so answer him honestly.

He'll explain." She turned to Doyle and moved behind him.

"My name is Doyle, I'm a private investigator and I'm investigating the murder of...well, I'll just say it...Tammy Gilpin."

Everyone expressed surprise except one person, a man sitting by himself at a table. Doyle made note to talk to him. "I'm sorry to just bring it up like that, but I don't have the luxury of time to find the killer."

The man sitting by himself said, "Why aren't the police investigating?"

Doyle moved closer to the man, "They are, but since her body was left in my backyard, I felt like finding out why. Did you know Tammy?"

He sat munching on an apple and then said, "I did. She was a loose woman. I just avoided her. Now she can deal with God, or Satan."

Oh great, a holy-roller type, Doyle thought. Doyle turned away from the man and gave his attentions to the rest of the people.

"I hope some of you were closer to Tammy than this man was." Doyle made a gesture to the man, wanting to give him the finger, but refrained. "What can you tell me about her and who she may have associated with outside of work?" Doyle focused his eyes on a blonde female looking very distressed. He moved closer to her. "Did you know Tammy very well?" he asked her.

She jumped and looked to the ground. "I...I did know her, we were sort of friends."

"Did she talk to you much about the men she hung out with?"

"Sorta," she said meekly.

"Well, did she or didn't she? It's not a difficult question," Doyle said firmly.

The girl looked up at Doyle and said, "She told me she liked picking up strangers, they didn't want to settle down like men she knew. She could have fun and they'd be gone the next day. I didn't think it was a good idea for her to do that. I told her it could be dangerous." She stopped talking and started crying softly.

Doyle turned to the manager and said, "Sally, could you take her to your office so she can be alone?"

The manager took the girl out as Doyle looked to the others. "Anyone else who can help me find her killer?"

The man who sat alone said, "You should talk to her boyfriend, the one who would pimp her out. He'll go to hell, too."

"Great, now you tell me. Who was her boyfriend?"

"I don't know who he was, but I heard them talking one day out in the furniture aisle. I was stacking mattresses and overheard them talking. He wanted her to go to the Glory Hole that night to meet a man he set up for her. He said the man would be a good customer."

Nice, Doyle thought, she was hooking, too. "Did he come here often?"

"I saw him a few times, but I never paid much attention to them," the lone man said.

Doyle's Justice

Doyle turned back to the group. "Anyone else see her with this mystery man?"

One boy held his hand up and said, "I think I saw them outside the front of the building one day. He was getting kinda mean with her. I thought about calling Sally, our manager, to see if Tammy needed any help. But they left before I could."

"So, no one knows who he is?" Doyle asked.

They all looked blank faced and said nothing.

"Fine, if you think of anything that may help, tell Sally and have her call me." He turned to the manager as she returned and handed her his card. "Thank you for your time, call if you have any word."

"I will," she replied and Doyle left the break room. He went out to his car and stood looking around. He was wondering who the mystery boyfriend was. Maybe Tammy's mother might know, but then she didn't care what her daughter did. He was getting hungry and it was getting late, so he drove to the nearest restaurant he could find and went in.

A bubbly girl of about twenty came bouncing over, really, she was bouncing, and gave Doyle a menu.

"Hi sir, today's special is meatloaf, but I wouldn't get it if I were you. It's not very fresh, so I would recommend the fish and chips. The fish is fresh and the fries are golden brown. Would you like a moment to think?"

Doyle was trying not to laugh and said, "Sure, I'll trust you. Give me the fish and chips. And a glass of Vernors if you have it."

"We sure do. I'll bring your drink right away." She zipped off and Doyle was thinking he was going to get sick of Vernors before the day was over. He really wanted a beer right now. Maybe he'd pick up a six pack and go back to the cabin to relax.

His drink and food came and it was good. If he stayed a few more days, he'd remember to come back here. He wasn't a good cook so he ate out a lot. He finished up his meal and left a generous tip for the girl. Hopefully, she'll remember him if he came back.

Sitting in his car he thought about going back to the Glory Hole. Maybe someone there would know who the mystery boyfriend was. It was getting darker, so the night-life should be starting in the bar. He drove over and parked. There were a few more cars than earlier, hopefully people who knew Tammy.

He went into the building and sat at the bar as an attractive barmaid came over to him. "Hey big, strong and handsome, what can I get you."

Doyle got a good laugh at that, which brightened his mood. "I don't know about the handsome part, but the big and strong of me will have a Miller."

"You got it, and you are definitely handsome," She smiled and went to get his beer. He watched her move, she was graceful and had a great body. Her tank top was low enough to view her bountiful breasts. He had to remember Val back in Detroit. Although he wasn't sure what their status really was,

Val never said she was exclusive with him, and he was definitely not ready to nest with one woman. But he wasn't the kind of man to cheat on a woman he was seeing, even without a commitment.

The woman came back and put his beer on the bar and said, "I'm Amber, and you are?"

"Doyle, Art Doyle," he replied.

"Is that like a 'Bond, James Bond' type of name? I suppose you're a secret agent, too."

He smiled, "No, but I am a private investigator."

"Hey, were you in here earlier asking about Tammy Gilpin?"

"The same person. You were here last night, right?"

"I was, and Tammy was in here with some guy I've never seen before. He was here waiting for her, then they hung around drinking and left about an hour later."

Doyle didn't see the man standing across the bar from him, watching and waiting.

*

Chapter 6

"Did Tammy spend a lot of time in here?" Doyle asked.

"She would come in and go to a man as if she knew him. They'd talk, drink, flirt and leave. The whole meeting would last only an hour or so, then they acted like they wanted to get out fast. I know she was whoring around, I felt sorry for her. She seemed like such a lonely girl when there weren't any men around. Some nights she would come in and sit drinking by herself. Sad."

Doyle thought back to when he spurned her affections, but was he just another man she wanted. He didn't know if she was after other men besides him. He never paid much attention to her. No reason to.

"I was told she had a boyfriend, or possibly a pimp, did you see anyone who may fit that description?"

"There was one man that would come in and talk to her briefly, then leave. But, I don't know what his relationship was with her. Any more questions, because I have a few questions of my own."

Doyle smiled and said, "Ask away."

"I get off at eleven, still enough time to shake a leg on the dance floor. Interested?"

Now Doyle was conflicted. He was so tempted, but he just couldn't. "I'm sorry, Amber. I'm spoken for and I don't think it would be fair to you."

"Who said I want fair? I just want to see if you can dance. But, if we were to do some horizontal dancing, that wouldn't be out of the question."

Doyle was about to answer when he heard *Jaws* playing in his pocket. Amber laughed and said "I may be dangerous, but I don't come with theme music."

Doyle laughed and took his phone out of his pocket. "Hello," he said when he saw there was no caller ID.

He heard, "Art, this is Mike, got two problems."

"That's one more than I have here," Doyle joked. "What's the first?"

"Well, we got another body. And you won't guess where it was found."

"I hope not by my cabin."

"Yep, right on the front porch, sitting in your chair."

"What the hell," he spat. "Any ID on the body?"

"Nope, but another note," Mike said and paused. Then he read, "*Doyle, he was ignored by you. You hurt his feelings. His death is on your hands.*"

Doyle couldn't believe what he heard. "Who found the body?"

"That's the other problem, he was found by an attractive woman who said she knew you."

"Who?" Doyle asked.

"She said her name is Val. Ring a bell?"

Now Doyle was in shock. "Are you at the cabin?"

"Of course, so is your lady friend and I think she's bordering on the edge of hysteria."

"Damn, I'll be there shortly," he said and hung up. He looked to Amber and said, "Sorry, I got another dead person to go identify." He downed the beer and put a ten on the counter.

"Stop back please, my offer will still be good," she said as Doyle smiled and headed out.

Bob Moats

On his way north to his cabin, his head was filled with all kinds of thoughts. Why was there another body left on his property and why was Val the one to find it? This was turning into an interesting night.

He arrived at his cabin about fifteen minutes later and parked on the lawn again. He saw Val's car parked up front and heard his name called.

"Art, come here." It was Val, sitting on the lawn clutching her purse. He went to her, kneeling.

"Are you all right?" he asked.

She sobbed, "No! Do you normally keep dead bodies on your property?"

"Not usually, but it seems to be a regular thing here lately. I have to go talk to my sheriff friend and find out what's happening. Stay here, I'll be back." He stood up and looked for Mike. He was on the porch with the coroner and his assistants. They looked like they were waiting for him.

He went to them and saw the body sitting so pleasantly on his wooden lawn chair. He was surprised the dead man didn't have a beer can in his hand.

"Hey, Mike. Still need me to ID the body?"

"If you can. He's a little fresher than poor Tammy. Elwood said he was murdered in the last two hours. We have no idea who he is. I didn't grow up with him, so you must have. You weren't a very nice kid were you?"

"Nope, I was a mean little cuss." Doyle went to the body as Mike shined his flashlight on the dead man's face. Doyle studied the face and said, "I hate to say it, but I'm not sure who he is. He looks familiar, but I can't place him. You'll have to run his prints."

Mike looked to Elwood and said, "You can take the body. I got all the photos I need, and if you could take prints, I'd appreciate it."

The assistants started to lift the man and stuff him in the black bag. Doyle said to Mike, "How did she let you know about the body?"

"She called 911 and they contacted my office, since it was out here. We got here and she was locked in her car. It took a little coaxing to get her to come out. You got a tough night ahead of you." Mike laughed.

Doyle gave a smirk to Mike and went back to Val. She was holding her knees and rocking. He sat on the grass next to her and put his arm around her. She stopped rocking and tucked in under his arm.

"What are you doing here?" Doyle asked her.

"I wanted to talk to you, but it can wait now."

Wanted to talk to me, Doyle thought. Last time he heard those words, Gwen moved away from him.

"Okay, take your time," he said, not really meaning it. He wanted to know what she had to tell him. He hated suspense.

They sat watching the coroner's men taking the body to the van. Mike came over and said, "I don't need you tonight, so I'll call you in the morning if we have confirmation on the fingerprints."

"Thanks, Mike. Did Elwood say how he died?"

"Oh, yeah, it looks like strangulation again. We have a serial killer, now."

Bob Moats

The name annoyed him. He had tracked down serial killers in Detroit and it still bothered him that a man could kill more than one person before he is caught. If he is caught. "If you need anything that I can provide from Detroit, let me know."

"I may need to bring in the FBI on this. If we have a serial killer, they're the ones who are equipped to handle it."

"You actually want to allow the FBI to take over? Most of the time police on a case don't like interference by the feebies," Doyle said.

"I know, but they do have profilers who can help to track this person down."

"Fine, but they better not get in my way. I'm going to find this scum and take him down. So call them if you feel you can't handle it," Doyle said with a smirk.

"I'll talk to you in the morning. Nice to meet you, Val, under the circumstances."

She nodded to him and was silent.

Mike left the front lawn and went back to his car. He drove out after the coroner's van.

Doyle started to stand. "Let's go in the cabin, it's too cold out here and the ground is damp." He helped her up and they went in. He turned up the heat to warm them, Val went to the couch and curled up with the blanket that was lying across the back.

He came to her and sat next to her. She was shivering, more from fright than the cold.

"It's over now. You came here to tell me something. How did you find the cabin?"

"Oscar made me a detailed map for finding you. I'm surprised he didn't call you," she said.

"Of course not, he wanted you to surprise me. And you got the surprise. Now Oscar is in trouble."

She shivered again and cuddled closer to Doyle. He spoke, "You said you had something to tell me? What is it?"

She sat up and pulled the blanket around her shoulders. She was avoiding the situation, Doyle thought. It was going to be bad news, he just felt it.

"Art, when we first met, I was working at the pool hall. When my ex got shot and killed, I got his life insurance. I'm very well set now with money. For years, I have always wanted to travel the world, especially to go to see New Zealand. After I saw the *Lord of the Rings* movie, I knew I had to go there. With all this money, I can now travel, but I'm sure you're not wanting to leave your job here. You wouldn't want to go with me, would you?"

Doyle sat thinking. He didn't really want to travel. He hated flying commercial airlines and wasn't interested in climbing mountains in New Zealand. He looked at her and then looked away. He couldn't tell her he didn't want to go and see her face.

He looked at his hands and said, "Val, I do care about you, but you know I'm not ready for a commitment. Traveling the world together is a commitment. So, I'm sorry, but I can't go. I do have a new firm to run, besides, what would Oscar and Marge do without me?"

"I was figuring that. So, shall we have one hell of a last night before I go?"

*

Chapter 7

Doyle woke the next morning feeling worn down a bit by Val and her exuberance during the night. He looked over and she wasn't in bed. He figured she was out making breakfast for herself. He got up and pulled on his pants, then went out to the main room. He looked over to the kitchen area and she wasn't there.

He went to the small dining table when he spotted a piece of paper. He picked it up and read, "*Art, thank you for the last month together. It was different, fun and I enjoyed it. I'm slipping out because I hate goodbyes. Thank you for everything, Val.*"

In his head he started singing that song by Gilbert O'Sullivan, "*Alone Again, Naturally*" and put the paper back down. Great, now he would have the song stuck in his head all day. Not that he wanted to be tied down to one woman anymore after his wife died, but it would be nice to have a relationship that lasted longer than a month. Although, he and Gwen were together for two and a half months.

Then he thought about Amber and her offer to do a dance or two. He knew he wasn't going to be able to stay here in his cabin for her, but it would be a good long distance relationship again. He was enjoying the vision of her, when he suddenly remembered the body on his porch.

The look on the face of the man stuck in his head, and it wasn't pleasant. The man's eyes were still open and staring straight ahead to see nothing anymore. He decided to get himself ready for the day and then call Mike to see if they got anything on the body.

He shaved and showered, then dressed in clean clothes. He went to the dining table and picked up his cellphone. He never had a phone line put in the cabin, he saw no need for it. He dialed Mike and waited.

"Hey Art," Mike's voice rang in Doyle's ear. "How did you make out with your lady friend? Did you comfort her?""

"She did a great job of comforting me. She drove up from the city to tell me she's going to be traveling the world, and gave me a goodbye night to remember for a long time."

"Lucky guy, I guess. We got a hit on the prints, want to know?"

"It's why I called. Talk to me."

"Well, his name is Harry Forman, he's from out by Hadley and he is…was, an insurance salesman. Sound familiar?"

Doyle suddenly remembered the man. "Yes, he kept bugging me to add more insurance to my policy because I was in a high risk job as a cop. I guess I kept putting him off and trying to ignore him. So that's where the note comes in saying that I ignored him. Wow, if every insurance salesman was murdered because people ignored them, there'd be a lot less of them."

"True. Now who would know enough about you that they would kill your acquaintances and former flames?"

"I honestly don't know. I don't have that many friends still back there in Oxford or up here in Metamora, other than yourself, so I'm not sure. Other than being up in my cabin, I haven't spent time in Oxford in over twenty years. I'll try and put together a list of people I still know who could be suspects."

"You should think about getting a big, vicious dog to tie up in your yard. Maybe it will keep serial killers away," Mike laughed.

"I may just sell the cabin and louse up the killer's plans. Since it seems like he is going to continue, I'll have to be more alert."

"I'll have a couple deputies cruise by every so often to watch for vehicles lurking around the area. It may deter the perp, but we still have to find him."

"I thought this could have been Tammy's mother, but this vic was too big for her to handle. So I'm stymied for now. There was some guy who was hanging around Tammy, but this is more aimed at me than a boyfriend wanting to murder Tammy and blame me. I'll give some thought as to who didn't like me and would want to pile bodies on my property."

"Let me know what you come up with. I'm holding off on calling the feds for now. But if we get another body, I'm calling the troops in."

Doyle's Justice

"Okay, I'll talk to you later," Doyle said and hung up. Now what will he do, he wondered. He stood and went outside for a breath of fresh air. The city smelled and wasn't very clean when it came to air, so it was good to come out here once in a while to clean out his lungs.

He stood on his porch staring at the chair where they found the body. He picked it up and moved it off the porch, bringing up another one from the front lawn. Not that there was anything wrong with the chair, but he was a little superstitious about things like that. He turned to look at the lake and saw movement off the left side of the shore. He didn't look right at it because he had good peripheral vision. The movement came again so he stepped off of the porch and walked towards the area.

Now he looked directly at the source of the movement and realized it was a human behind the bushes. He started running towards the intruder, which caused the person to run. Doyle followed him along the shore until the person cut into the woods. Doyle followed as fast as he could, but the person seemed in better shape. Finally, the intruder tripped on a branch on the ground and went down. Doyle pulled his .38 from behind him and aimed it at the form on the ground. The person turned and looked shocked at seeing the gun.

Doyle was surprised to see it was just a boy, about sixteen or so. The boy looked frightened. "Get up, slowly," Doyle ordered.

The boy pushed himself up and stood. He put his hands up in the air, Doyle told him to put them down.

"Now, explain to me why you were spying on me?" Doyle commanded.

"I'm sorry, Mr. Doyle, but I wanted to see a real life private eye. I've only seen them on TV."

"How did you know who I was?"

"I met a guy who told me. He said who you were and asked me to watch you."

"Who's the guy?"

"Just some man who comes into the grocery store where I work at as a stock boy. I've only seen him around a couple times, he said he was from some bureau of investigations and wanted me to report on your activities. He said you could be a terrorist."

Doyle would have laughed, but the kid was serious. "I'm a former Detroit homicide detective. and now I'm a private eye. So, I'm not a terrorist. Do you think this man will come back to find out what you know?"

"He said he would be back to get my report."

"How long have you been watching me?"

"Just since this morning. I saw that beautiful woman leave earlier and then I saw you come out." The boy started to shiver. Doyle figured it was the cold. Doyle wasn't wearing his jacket, and now that he wasn't running, he was feeling the cold, also. He put his gun away and told the boy, "Come with me, you must be freezing. I'll make you something warm to drink."

They went back down the shore as the boy was asking questions about Doyle being a cop. "That must have been exciting, being a cop in Detroit. I'd like to be a cop when I get old enough."

"There's more to being a cop than just joining. They make you go through physical testing and exams to see how smart you are. You have to go through an academy before you can become a cop. I don't recommend it, unless you are really sure and ready to put yourself through a lot of work and pain." He was spreading it on a little thick, but he didn't want the boy to get his hopes up. He was on the small side, and a bit thin. He'd have to meet minimum requirements to get in the academy.

They arrived back at the cabin and went in. Doyle told the boy to sit near the heating vent and went to put on his jacket. He went to the kitchen area and wondered what he could make that would warm them both up. He opened the fridge and didn't see much. He looked in the cupboards and found some instant chocolate mix. He must have bought it long ago, but it should still be good. He heated some water and made the chocolate as the boy sat watching him. "What's your name?" Doyle asked.

"Jeff Kennedy, sir," he answered.

"What grocery store do you work at?" Doyle asked as he poured the mixture in a couple cups. He handed one to the boy who thanked him politely.

"The one on the corner of Pratt and Baldwin."

Doyle knew the one, he went there a number of times to get supplies. "So, this man doesn't come around a lot?"

"No, I've only seen him a couple of times. He asked me if I knew you, I said I didn't. He told me your name and where you lived and asked me to keep an eye on you."

"Could you give the sheriffs a description of the man, so they could do a sketch of his face?"

"Do you think he's a bad man?"

"Well, there have been two murders in the last two days, so he might be involved. And, I expect you to be careful. If it is him, you could be in danger too."

*

Chapter 8

"Wow," the boy said, his eyes growing wide. "Do you think I need protection, or should I carry a gun?"

"No, you don't need to carry a gun," Doyle said. "They're dangerous unless you know what you're doing. Have you ever fired a gun or a rifle before?"

The boy put down his empty cup and said, "No, never. My dad forbid me to ever use a gun."

"Wise man," Doyle said, finishing up his drink.

"My dad was killed in Iraq. By a gun, they said."

Doyle suddenly felt bad. He stood and told the boy to follow. They went out and over to the side of the property where Doyle had large bales of hay stacked up. In front of the bales was a single bale with a target attached to it. The target was printed with a figure of a man. Doyle said, "Cover your ears."

He quickly drew his .38 and fired three consecutive shots. The boy jumped even though he had his hands over his ears. Doyle brought the weapon down, put the safety on and looked to the boy. "Loud, isn't it?" Then he walked to the target, the boy following. He pulled the target off the bale and showed the boy the three closely grouped holes at center mass right in the man's chest, made by the bullets.

"These holes could be in a person's body and kill that person. This is why you don't need a gun. Unless you're a cop."

Jeff said, "Wow, can I keep this?"

Doyle smiled and said he could. Jeff rolled the target instead of folding it. Doyle took Jeff back to the cabin. "Relax on the couch while I call a sheriff friend of mine."

Jeff went to the couch and unrolled the target, studying the shot grouping. Doyle pulled his cell phone out and called Mike. After a few rings he came on. "Did you solve the case yet?" Mike asked.

"No, but I got a lead. I have a boy here in my cabin who was asked by a man to spy on me and report what I was up to. The boy said the man approached him in the store he works at and lied about me being a terrorist. He asked the kid to watch me. I think if you could set up a sting for when the man comes back to get the info from the boy, you could nab him."

"I'll be right out, keep him there." Mike hung up.

Doyle pulled a kitchen chair over to the boy and sat, straddling the chair backwards. "Did the man say when he was coming back for your reports on me?"

Bob Moats

"He told me yesterday he'd be back tomorrow morning. It's when I work again," Jeff explained.

"Good, you're going to be part of an undercover police sting. You will go about your business stocking and there will be officers in and around the building watching for the man. When he shows, they will hold him for questioning. Think you could do that?"

"I'd be part of a police operation, sure, I could do it," he said excitedly.

Ten minutes later, Mike showed up and Doyle introduced them as Mike sat next to Jeff.

"Tell me everything that happened with this man," Mike asked.

The boy related all that happened with the stranger and described him. Mike looked to Doyle and said, "Think it's wise to involve Jeff in this? It could be dangerous."

"I could handle myself," Jeff protested.

"I'm sure you could, sport, but we don't want to take any unnecessary chances," Mike said. "We'll have people all around you, and if you are told to move, you better move away quickly. If there's any gun fire, drop to the ground and stay down. I'll have to talk to your boss to arrange for this to happen. You said he would come in tomorrow?"

"That's what he told me yesterday. My next shift is in the morning," he said.

Mike looked to Doyle and said, "There's one problem. If he's from around here, as I suspect he is, he'll know my deputies and me. It will be hard to have them in the store without him seeing them."

Doyle thought about it, then said, "Hold on, I'm calling in the cavalry." He pulled his phone and called Oscar. Oscar answered the phone and said, "Oscar Drew Investigations."

"Very funny, Oscar. I need you up here tonight. We have a sting in the morning to catch a killer. Are you involved in anything?"

"Nope, I just finished following a cheating husband. I can be there in an hour and a half. I'll need to get a change of clothes."

"That works. Take two hours, I don't want you rushing on the freeway. I'll see you then," Doyle said, then hung up. "My partner isn't from around here and he was a homicide cop, too," he told Mike.

"Good, we can have Oscar near the boy, and hide my men outside in a van. We'll wire the boy to be sure."

"A wire!" Jeff exclaimed. "I like that. Like on the cop shows."

"Yes, just like that. Now, we need to go to the store after Oscar gets here, to plot out the scene. I want to be sure Jeff has plenty of exits in case of trouble."

One hour and fifteen minutes later, Oscar showed up. Doyle looked at his watch and said, "I hope you didn't speed."

"Nah, I know all the shortcuts. So what's up?"

Doyle introduced Oscar to Mike and Jeff, and then he explained the last two days and told him the plan for the next morning.

"I'm a little too old to be a stockboy, but I could be a customer wandering around."

"That should work. We need to go to the store and talk to the owner so he'll know what we are doing. I don't think he'd like gunplay in his store if it happens," Doyle said.

"Lead the way, oh great hero," Oscar said and smiled at Jeff. "You come with me, I'll protect you from harm."

Jeff grinned widely and followed Oscar. The men went out to their cars and drove the short distance to the store. It was basically like a general store, an old building in need of a facelift. They parked on the side and went in. Jeff went in the back room and brought out the owner.

"This is Mr. Franzella, he's the owner of the store."

Mike smiled and said, "How are you today, Emile?"

The man smiled back and said, in slightly broken English as he was French, "I'm fine, Michael, are you here on business?" He looked at Jeff and continued, "Has Jeffrey caused problems?"

"No, Emile, but it is serious. Emile, this is Art Doyle and his partner Oscar Drew. They are private investigators and are helping the sheriff with a couple murders."

"Murders? That's not good. Who was murdered?"

"One woman from Oxford and a man from over by Hadley. I'm sure you don't know them. But the problem is, we think the killer may have talked to Jeff yesterday and is coming back to talk again in the morning."

"A killer in my store? Not good, not good at all."

"Well, we want to stop him, but we need to have the man come in to talk to Jeff, then we will arrest him. So, with your permission, may we use the store to stop this killer?"

"But of course. You need to get this man off the streets. What do you need me to do?"

They walked Franzella through the store explaining what would happen. Then they studied the layout for the best place to have Jeff working. Oscar checked out the aisles and recommended the bread aisle. It was narrow and yet had an opening to the back room if Jeff had to run. They all agreed and Franzella said he'd have a supply of bread to put out.

Franzella asked, "Jeffrey, Does your mama know you are doing this?"

Jeff looked at the sheriff, Mike said, "I'll talk to her and explain. Now, we should get out of here in case the killer comes around and sees us together."

They all said their goodbyes and Mike took Jeff to go see his mother. "I'll caution her about what we are going to do and explain we'll have plenty of backup," he told Doyle before they left.

They drove off and Oscar said, "Okay, what's fun to do around this town at night."

Doyle smiled and said, "Feel like dancing?"

"I'm not the best dancer, but if you feel the need, I'll go along. Say, where's Val?"

"Oh yeah, I've got a story to tell you and a small bone to pick."

They were back in the cabin, Oscar was sitting on the couch. "I can't believe she left you to go traveling the world. You could have gone with her, you know."

"No thanks, I'm not into traveling the world anymore. I had enough of that on the FBI Terrorist Task Force. She's better off this way. She got what she always wanted and it didn't include me. Besides, if I left you in charge, the business would be closed in a month."

"Well, maybe two weeks," Oscar mugged. "So, tell me about this barmaid you met last night. Is she another hottie?"

"Yeah, I would say she is. But I don't know if I want to start another relationship so soon after Val leaving."

"Yeah, tell me another. Let's go dancing." Oscar said, "You want me to drive my car, in case you go off with the hottie?"

Doyle stood and got his keys, then stood there thinking, "Okay, you drive. But remember where you leave me in case I need a ride."

On the car ride over, Doyle was thinking. "I don't think we need to stay out late tonight, we have to go watch Jeff in the morning. I'm not good at functioning that early after a night of partying."

"I'll keep you in line, don't worry."

"That's what worries me," Doyle grinned.

*

Chapter 9

Oscar pulled into the parking lot, the place was busy. He found an empty space and pulled in, then they went to the entrance and entered. It was busy inside and Doyle spotted Amber behind the bar. He nudged Oscar and pointed her out.

"Hell, you have a way of attracting hotties," Oscar said. There were two stools open at the bar, so they sat. Amber glanced down and saw Doyle. She gave him a wave and a wink.

Oscar said, "I hope you two don't start acting goofy tonight or I'm leaving you here and going back to drink cheap beer at the cabin."

"I'm not planning on getting lucky tonight, we have work in the morning. But, I can set up something for later," Doyle said.

"You better be careful not to get too close to her, your stalker might make her a victim."

"Don't even joke about that. I'm not wanting any more bodies. Least of all hottie barmaids." He laughed and said, "Let's just have a good time. We've never done this before."

"We've been too busy chasing cheating spouses and finding missing persons. You were also busy with Val, so we never got together."

"I'm sorry, Oscar. We'll have to have dates more often."

"Can you call it something other than a date? That sounds so weird."

Amber finally found some time to come down to them. "Let me get you your drinks before I get busy again."

Doyle and Oscar ordered and she went off to get their beers. "This one is on me. For having to leave earlier to go check out a body," she said to Doyle.

"Amber, this is Oscar Drew, my partner in my investigating business. Oscar, this is Amber."

"Nice to meet you," Oscar said. "Do you have any single, good-looking friends?"

"I know a couple guys who are single, good-looking, and are my friends."

Oscar gave her a surprised look. She said, "You really need to be more specific with me. I'm sure you meant single, women friends. Yes, I do. They'll be here later." She grinned at Doyle and went off.

Oscar turned to Doyle and said, "She's a keeper."

Around eleven o'clock, Amber came up to Doyle and pulled him off his stool. "Time to dance, and the band is playing the song that I requested." The song was '*I'll Still Be Loving You*' by Restless Heart. It was a very slow tune and Amber snuggled up close. She put her arms around his neck and moved her head to his ear, giving it a kiss. He tensed up from the chill he got from her kiss. She laughed.

"Are you afraid of me?" she asked.

"Oh hell no, I'm just surprised you move so fast."

"I don't waste time. So sailor, what are you doing later?"

"After the dance, I'll explain."

"I have a feeling I'm not going home with you."

Doyle thought on that. "Well, if you are coming to my place, it could be arranged. I'll explain."

They danced to the song and the next, it was slow also. Doyle figured she arranged it, so she could rub up against him. He didn't mind.

Doyle looked next to him and saw Oscar on the dance floor with a woman. She wasn't bad looking either. Amber whispered in his ear, "That's Marie, she's one of my good-looking, single friends. I told her to hit on your friend."

Doyle laughed and said, "Thank you."

They sat back down on the stools and were relaxing when a bald-headed man in a black leather vest came up to Amber and grabbed her arm. "Let's dance," he growled.

Amber pulled her arm away and said to get lost. He grabbed her again and started to pull. Doyle stood and moved to the man. "The lady said to get lost."

"Who are you, her father?" He was drunk and stunk of liquor.

"Move on, friend," Doyle said.

"Are you going to move me?"

"I may if you don't get out of our sight. That's your first warning," Doyle said.

The man gave Doyle a push on his shoulder.

"That's *your* first warning, pal," the man said. Then the man raised his fist to strike. Doyle moved his head, the punch completely missing him, then

Bob Moats

Doyle came up into his ribs with both his fists. The man staggered back holding his breath, then he lunged back at Doyle, trying to grab him. Doyle spun around and planted his fist into the man's throat. That took the man down. Doyle quickly pulled a plastic zip-cuff from his pocket, and while the man was trying to recover from the punch to his throat, Doyle pulled his arms behind him and strapped the band around his wrists. Lots of training cuffing perps as a cop gave him the speed to do so.

The man was spitting on the floor, clearing his throat, as Doyle and Oscar pulled him up and put him in a booth. Doyle told Amber to call the sheriff, he was pressing charges. He wanted Amber to call to make it more official.

About twenty minutes later, the bully was taken away. Doyle told the deputy to throw him in the drunk tank for the night, then let him go. The deputy smiled and said, "I'll tell Mike you were brawling in the bar."

Doyle laughed and said to do that. The deputy took the brute away and Doyle went back to Amber. "My hero, do you always get into a fight in a bar?"

"Not often." He turned to see a monster of a man in a black t-shirt that read '*Black Sabbath*' across the front. The man had to be about three hundred pounds and was probably about six feet around his waist. Great, Doyle thought, a buddy of the brute. Before Doyle could do anything, the man grabbed him around his arms and shoulders in a bear hug and lifted him up. Oscar was up and waiting to see what would happen.

Doyle's Justice

The man shook Doyle up and down and said out loud, "Doyle, it's so good to see you, you old slimeball."

Doyle was now wondering who this mountain of a man was. He put Doyle down and said. "You don't remember me, do you? You arrested me down in Detroit at the Grandy in 1984 for drunk and disorderly. You took me down in seconds. I was amazed."

Doyle suddenly remembered the man. "Hector, isn't it?"

"You got it, chief. What are you doing up here? I'm with the band, I'm the drummer."

"I used to live up here. But I'm still in Detroit as a P.I. now."

"Cool, dude. I live off Livernois in the city. Where's your office?"

"Michigan and Trumbull, in a strip mall."

"I'll have to look you up. Sorry man, I have to go back to drumming. Talk another time." The huge man turned and went back to the stage.

Doyle sat back down. Amber leaned to him and said, "You have such an interesting life. Do you ever have quiet times?"

"Only when I sleep," Doyle said.

"Well, I'll have to watch you sleep some night soon." She grinned.

"Let's go to the booth and I'll explain my morning tomorrow." He nodded to Oscar who was busy talking to the other woman. Doyle and Amber went to the booth and sat. Doyle explained the events of the last couple days and the plan for the sting in the store.

"Well, I hope you get the man. You're just like one of those detectives on TV."

"Except they get paid better than I do," he said with a smile. Amber leaned into him and gave him a kiss on his lips. He felt the chill running up his spine that he always felt when a woman kissed him.

"You mentioned that going to your place would be better for us?" she asked.

"I wouldn't have to rush getting out of bed to hurry back to my place, I'd already be there."

"I don't work tomorrow, so I could hang around until you get back."

"I think it would be better if you left with me, considering there's a killer who knows where my cabin is. I don't want to come back to find you dead in my bed."

She thought about that. "We could leave together. What about your friend?"

"Oscar sleeps on the pull out couch, you aren't loud, are you?"

"No, but my friend is," she grinned, looking over to Oscar and the woman. Now Doyle was wishing he had a bigger place.

An hour later, the four of them entered the cabin carrying a case of beer. They all sat talking about crime in the big city. Oscar was feeling good and kept grinning at Doyle. Doyle told him to stop it.

Seven o'clock the next morning, Doyle woke feeling good, yet a little bad. Val had only left him twenty-four hours ago. He didn't know if there was a proper amount of time to mourn over the break-up with a woman, but this would make up for the loss. He woke everyone and said they had work to do. Doyle went outside to call Mike and find out if his talk with the mother went well.

"It's all set. I've got the surveillance van ready to go. We'll all have wireless ear buds so we can communicate, and I've got Jeff in to get wired. You and Oscar should come to the station and we'll all go in the van."

"Works for me. What time does the store open?"

"Jeff said he has to be there at eight-thirty to start setting up before they open at nine. So be here by eight."

They agreed and hung up. He felt someone come up behind him and put arms around his body. She kissed his neck and whispered, "Will I see you later?"

"If all goes well and I don't get shot, you will."

*

Chapter 10

He turned to her, "Is your friend awake?"

"Well, she's not exactly a friend. More of an acquaintance. She hangs around the bar a lot. Kind of like Tammy was."

"Ah, a loose woman. Oscar's type of female. Get her moving, we have to go."

Amber laughed and said, "I'll go roust her out of bed." She went back into the building. Doyle looked out at the lake, it was calm, the way Doyle hoped the day would go. Oscar came out all dressed and ready to leave.

"Well, you are rubbing off on me when it comes to women. I guess I'll keep you around," Oscar said.

"That's nice of you. We need to be heading over to the sheriff's office to start our sting. Is your girlfriend up?"

"I wouldn't call her my girlfriend, she can sure drink. She's still passed out."

"Well, they'll have to get themselves out. We need to go." Doyle went in and found Amber trying to get Marie to sit up. "We have to go work, get her awake, and when you leave, lock up the cabin."

She gave him a kiss and said she would take care of it. Doyle went out and said to Oscar, "Follow me to the sheriff's office. We'll take both cars, just in case."

They drove out and arrived shortly after. Doyle saw the van that they would hide in while they watched the store. It was an older vehicle and had rust growing on the lower portions of it. He thought about the undercover vans they used in Detroit, all shiny and new. This one would look less like a cop vehicle. Oscar came up to him and they went in.

The main room was busy with men working around Jeff to get him set up to work his first undercover assignment. A woman was standing by, probably his mother. Mike saw Doyle and came over.

"We're ready to take this guy down. Hopefully he shows," Mike said.

"Well, we have all day to wait. Are we ready to go?" Doyle asked.

"Just waiting for you."

"Is that the mother, and is she going along?"

"Yep, since Jeff is a minor, we need a parent to be with us. Just touching all bases."

"Okay, we're ready. I'm having Oscar drive his car over to look like a customer. It would be funny to have a man in the store and not have a car out front."

"Good thinking, let's go," Mike said.

Mike herded everyone into the van and put Jeff by the door to let him out first. The deputy driving was dressed down for the occasion, warm jacket and baseball cap. He drove over and pulled alongside of the store. Mike told Jeff to jump out and go in quickly so no one saw him. Jeff obeyed and was gone.

They had given Jeff an ear bud so he could hear them talking. Mike tested the unit by asking Jeff to say something.

"Agent X1 reporting to base. Do you read me?" Jeff said.

Everyone laughed and Mike said, "Coming in clearly, Agent X1. Now, don't talk to us unless we ask you a question."

Jeff said, "I'll go radio silent, base. Over."

Doyle figured the kid was enjoying this. Too bad he wasn't aware of how dangerous the situation was. They waited until the store opened and they watched through the darkened window of the van as Oscar get out of his beat up Chevy and went in.

They sat waiting for the man to show up. A few people came and went to buy groceries, but none approached the boy. They had waited about an hour when a young boy rode up on his bike and went in the store.

"What's happening, Oscar?" Doyle asked into the microphone.

Oscar replied, "I'm not sure, the new kid coming in went to Jeff and handed him an envelope. Now the kid is leaving. I'll go get the envelope and check it out."

Oscar went slowly down the aisle and came by Jeff. He looked around and since there was no one else in the store, he asked Jeff for the envelope. Jeff said it was addressed to Mr. Doyle.

Doyle heard that and felt something was very wrong. "What does it say, Oscar?" he spoke into the mic.

They could hear the envelope being torn open, then silence as Oscar was reading the contents. They heard Oscar curse. "Damn it, the killer knew about us. Hold on," he read aloud, '*Doyle, thanks for being so patient to wait for me, but I'm not coming. You fell for my little ruse, now who's the smarter one? And thanks for giving me a new person to kill.*' That's all it says."

Doyle burst out of the van and yelled, "Oscar, get out here now!"

Mike went after Doyle and asked, "What's up?"

"The bastard made us sit here waiting for him," Doyle yelled. "He planned it. I have to go back to my cabin. I have a bad feeling."

Oscar came running out of the store. Doyle told Mike to follow, but to leave a deputy to watch Jeff and his mother. "I'm going to my cabin, follow quickly."

Doyle and Oscar went to Oscar's car and he peeled out of the parking lot heading back to the cabin.

"Damn it, he rubbed my nose in it. Son-of-a-bitch. If he did what I think happened, we have a problem," Doyle lamented.

"You're not thinking Amber and Marie?" Oscar asked.

"I hope not, move faster!"

They pulled down the dirt drive to the cabin and Doyle was out before Oscar even stopped. He saw Amber's car still in the drive and he ran to the front and stopped. He turned away as Oscar came running up and saw Marie's body on the porch sitting up against the building.

"Art, what about Amber?" Oscar said.

Doyle ran up to the door and opened it. He looked in and didn't see her. He checked the bedroom, it was empty. He went back out to Oscar, looking sick over Marie. "She's not here. Her car is still in the drive, so he's got her with him."

Mike was just pulling in the drive and Doyle ran to him. "Put out a bulletin to search every car, van, and truck around the area, the bastard has Amber."

"Amber from the Glory Hole?" Mike asked.

"The same, make the call."

Mike pulled on his radio and made a call for a complete dragnet of all vehicles in the area, coming and going out of Baldwin Road and vicinity. He looked back to Doyle who was pacing.

"Damn, if I had made them leave when we did, this wouldn't have happened," Doyle said.

Oscar said, "You couldn't have known. This guy had to have been watching your cabin to see what was going on. He knew the girls didn't go with us. He must have got the jump on them right after we left."

"Then he wrote the letter and found some kid to deliver it. There's kids all over the place, so it wouldn't be hard to find one." He turned to Mike, "Did anyone think to stop the kid on the bike?"

"Yeah, I had one of my deputies stop him down the road from the store. He's going back to the station for questioning now."

"Get a description of the man, and find out if he saw the vehicle he was driving," Doyle said.

Doyle stood thinking. "I don't think he'll harm Amber. He may keep her to make me crazy. He must have seen us in the bar last night and even followed us to the cabin."

"Makes sense to me," Oscar said, glancing up to Marie, thinking about what they shared last night. He was getting madder now. "We have to step up and get this guy, Art. Is there anyone in your past that has a vendetta on you?"

Doyle looked at his partner and frowned. "I've left a lot of people in my wake. Could be any number of them."

They turned when they saw the coroner's van pull in. Elwood came to Doyle and said, "I could just put a morgue here, if you don't mind."

"Can you tell me how she died?" Doyle asked bluntly.

Elwood nodded and went to the body. He kneeled down and studied it for a moment. He stood and said to Doyle standing off the porch, "She was strangled like the rest. But, I noticed a blunt trauma mark on her head. I'd say he knocked her out first, then strangled her. I'll know more after I get her back into autopsy."

"Thanks, Doc." He looked at Oscar. "He must have slipped up onto the porch, and when they were coming out, he hit Marie, then either hit Amber or he may have had a gun. I'm just speculating." He took a walk over to the porch and saw a wooden mallet from a croquet game that was left from the original cabin owners leaning against the side of the building. He went to it and called for Mike.

"Doc said it looked like she was hit on the head first, before being strangled. This may be the weapon."

Mike called one of his deputies and told him to take the mallet in for prints. The deputy put on gloves and picked up the mallet, taking it to a car.

"What are you going to do now, Art?" Mike asked.

"I'm going to stop this bastard. I don't need this crap."

*

Chapter 11

Marie's body was taken away by the coroner's men, and Mike was scouting around the property looking for anything that might help. Doyle was in his cabin going over the place to see if anything would pop for him. He did notice that both of the women's purses were still on the bed, so they weren't leaving when the perp attacked them. Doyle tried to visualize the scene as it could have happened.

Oscar was standing in the open door watching Doyle prowl around the room. Doyle reminded Oscar of the TV detective "Monk" with his hand gestures, recreating the crime.

"Getting anything?" Oscar asked.

Doyle stood looking frustrated and not liking it. "I can't be sure how he attacked the women. He may have had a gun and came in, threatening them. That mallet he used on Marie that was standing out by the side of the cabin, it was inside here last time I saw it. Over in that corner," he said pointing. "Maybe he got them to both sit on the bed, then took the mallet and hit Marie with it. I'm sure Amber would have moved away, but he had to have had a gun to control her. He may have tied up Amber then staged Marie outside for us to find her."

"Why would he put the mallet outside and not leave it in here?"

Doyle thought on that, "Good question. Maybe he was going to use it on Amber but she managed to run outside, he followed and dropped the mallet out there."

"Well, this guy is thorough with his kills. He loves you and likes giving you his little presents," Oscar said. "I hope he's not saving Amber for his next kill."

"Yeah, I thought about that, too. I've been thinking about a couple men that I helped to put away in prison that lived in this area, we need to check to see their prison status. I'll give you a list and you can get on your computer to hack into the DPD databases to see. You still can get in, right?"

"Yep, so far they haven't caught me. I have my laptop in the car, but you don't have Wi-Fi out here, so I'll have to check when we get back to town."

"We need to go back to get my car, you can check then," he said as Mike entered the cabin.

"Nothing unusual outside, he was careful not to leave any footprints or marks. I could see where he must have brushed the ground to hide his tracks. Not much more to do out there. What are you going to do now?" Mike asked.

"Oscar and I are going back to get my car, then we have a project to do. May we borrow an unused room at your station?"

"Sure, you can use the conference room. I'll meet you back there." He went out and Doyle followed with Oscar ahead of him. They got in their vehicles and drove back to the station.

Doyle asked as they entered the building, "Did they get anything from the kid on the bike?"

"I'm about to find out. They got the kid in that room," he said pointing. "We had to wait until his mother came in before we could talk to him, he's a minor."

Mike, Doyle and Oscar entered the small interrogation room as the boy looked back to what must have been his mother. Mike spoke first, "Mrs. Rollings, your son has done no wrong, but he may have information that would help us catch a murderer."

She looked stressed and said "Is my son in danger?"

Doyle spoke, "We doubt very seriously that any harm will come to your son. We just need to ask a few questions, if it's all right with you."

She agreed and Doyle went to sit next to the boy. "What's your name, son?"

"Walter," he said quietly.

"Well, Walt, a man gave you an envelope to take to Jeff in the store, is that correct?"

He nodded his head.

"Can you tell us what the man looked like?"

The boy sat thinking and making faces, like he was constipated. They gave him time, he finally said, "He was as tall as that man," he said pointing to Mike. "He had dark hair, but he was wearing a baseball hat, his hair looked long. He had a moustache and was wearing sunglasses."

Doyle realized that the man had disguised himself. "Did he have a car or a van?"

"Not that I saw, he was standing by the road just before the store. I was going there to get some milk for mom, when he came out of the woods. He stopped me and asked if I would give an envelope to Jeff. He asked if I knew Jeff, I said I did. He gave me some money to deliver the envelope. I did, but forgot to get the milk."

"Well, I'm sure the sheriff will have someone take you to get the milk. Thank you, Walt, it was a big help," Doyle said.

"I did good?" he asked.

"Yes, you did good," Doyle said, not wanting to hurt the boy's feelings. He stood up and turned to Oscar. "Get your laptop, we have some hunting to do."

Oscar grinned and went out. Doyle asked Mike if they had Wi-Fi, he said they did. "Good, Oscar is going to check on a couple criminals I put away." Doyle and Mike followed Oscar out. Mike called for one of his deputies to take the boy and his mother to the store. Doyle turned to the Deputy and handed him a twenty. "Get both of them some treats, candy, hot dog, or a pastry, whatever, and pay for their milk." The deputy took the bill and went to get the boy and his mother.

Mike took Doyle to the conference room and said, "Is Oscar going to be able to get info on your past arrests?"

"I'm sure he'll be able to find the status of my past criminals."

"I can run anyone in prison through my system," Mike offered.

"I'll give you a copy of my list, so we can cover all bases." Doyle sat down and took his note pad out, writing the names of the men he helped put away. He doubled the list, one for Oscar and one for Mike.

Oscar came back in and set up his laptop. "What's the passcode for your Wi-Fi?" Oscar asked Mike.

Mike gave him a blank look and then called for someone named Paul. A young man in uniform came in and Mike said to help Oscar. "He's the geek here and set up the Wi-Fi for us, he'll help you."

Paul got Oscar hooked up to the internet and then Mike gave him the list of criminals and told him to run them. Paul went out as Oscar hooked up to the DPD database. Doyle handed Oscar the list and after the database came up, Oscar started to enter the names.

About fifteen minutes later, Oscar gave his report. "Okay, this guy named Greg Pender is still doing time for murder, but he would have been a good suspect. The next, Ken Reed, is also doing time as were the next two after him. The only one who was paroled in the last month was Reid Walling. He's from this area, and is listed by his parole officer as still being here."

"I remember Walling, real bad dude," Mike said. "We had lots of problems with him in days past, but he hasn't been heard from in a while. Where does it say he's living now?" Mike asked Oscar. Oscar read the address as Mike wrote it down. "Shall we go visit our parolee?"

Paul came in and gave Mike a sheet of paper with the information he got from his database. Mike looked at it and thanked Paul.

Doyle, Oscar and Mike went out of the building to the cars. "What did Paul come up with?" Doyle asked.

"Same as Oscar got. I think the databases are all interconnected. Are you sure this is all the men you put away?"

"Those that lived in this area, yes. But I'm not including all the men I locked up from Detroit. This could be a nightmare."

"Well, let's check on Walling and go from there," Mike said. They got into their cars, Oscar went with Doyle in the Charger, and drove out.

"How you hanging in?" Oscar asked Doyle.

"Not well. I hope Walling is the man. If not, I may just beat on him for the hell of it. For old time's sake." Doyle smiled.

"What are you going to do when we get there? We don't have a warrant."

"As I've said before, we're not cops. I may find a reason to enter his house, then Mike can come in."

"Works for me," Oscar said as they got near the address. It was a lonely stretch of road, and the houses were spread out widely. They found the address and pulled into the drive. There was a van in front of a rundown garage. The van was a wreck itself, and looked like it couldn't move. The house was really rundown also. The paint was peeling and the windows had broken shades and threadbare curtains. It looked like a haunted house. Doyle considered Walling and thought the house was perfect for him.

They parked and went to the door. The porch sagged and was creaking badly. Doyle stepped on a board and it broke through. He pulled his foot up before he sunk into the depths of the hole. They carefully went to the door and Doyle banged on it.

A few minutes later they heard a voice. "What is it, this better be good." Then the door flew open and there stood Reid Walling.

*

Chapter 12

"What the hell! Doyle, you better have a good reason to be bothering me," he yelled out the door at the men. "I did my time, there's no reason you need to harass me."

Mike stepped forward and said, "We aren't harassing you. We need to know where you've been the last couple days."

"Why? Is someone dead and you think I did it? You want to know where I've been, hold on." He opened the door and stepped out. He went to the edge of the porch just as a siren blared out. He stepped back and the noise stopped. He pulled his pant leg up and showed them an electronic tether. "My parole officer doesn't trust me. Does that answer your question? I haven't left my house in over a month."

"How do you get your food?" Doyle asked.

"I have it delivered. Now, can I go back to my TV? It's all I have now, because of you." He moved back to the door.

"Walling, you deserved what you got, with or without me. You are a lowlife criminal and should've been put away for life. Too bad Michigan doesn't have the death penalty, I'd be there to pull the switch for your execution, or however they would do it. You are not worth worrying about. Why don't I believe you? I'm sure you can work that tether to your advantage."

Doyle busted in past Walling. He looked around the living room and went into the kitchen. "Where's the basement, Walling?" he yelled at the man.

"You can't do this, where's your warrant?" Walling protested.

"I'm not a cop anymore. I don't need one, so sue me. Where's the basement?" he yelled.

Oscar came up behind the two men facing each other. Oscar was ready to protect his partner. Mike came up behind the men, now inside, because Doyle entered the house. Probable cause.

"You find it, asshole," Walling said.

Doyle went through the house and found a door to the basement. He called to Mike and asked him to stay at the top of the stairs with Oscar. Doyle went down in the basement, it was musty and dark. He found a switch on the wall and turned it on. The room lit up brightly, more than a basement needed for light. He looked over and saw the table, it had blood on it. On a separate table were surgical tools, all covered in blood. He looked around and found garbage bags tied up tight. He felt around the bags and knew exactly what was in them. Body parts.

Doyle ran back to the stairs and yelled up, "Oscar, gun on Walling, now." He heard nothing. Doyle slowly went up the stairs with his Sig pulled. He came to the door and peeked around the corner where he saw Oscar and Mike holding their hands up in the air. Behind them was Walling with a shotgun. Doyle had a clear shot, so he didn't hesitate, he brought his gun up and fired.

Walling screamed and spun around. He turned, still holding on to the shotgun aimed at the men. Mike and Oscar pulled their weapons and turned, firing at Walling. It was overkill, but it was effective.

An hour later, Mike had his men in going through the house, and Elwood was examining the body parts.

"It's going to take forever to identify these people," Elwood said.

"You can check with our missing person's database," Mike said. "Hopefully, it will help. Sorry, Doc, but that's life."

"No, that's death. Just how did Walling get all these people in here to mutilate?"

"I don't know," Mike said, "but if you can get an ID on even one of the bodies, we can find out what the link is to Walling."

"I'll do my best. This is sick," he said looking at the three bags of body parts. "I'll take these back and start my autopsies. Give me some time." He called to his men to come down and take the bags out.

Doyle was standing, looking at the body of Walling as Mike came up. "Maybe we shouldn't have blasted him. He may have given us some information," Doyle said.

"No, he wouldn't have," Mike said. "I remember him being tight-lipped in the past. I've got cadaver dogs coming from the State Police to search around the property for more bodies. Never can tell."

"Worth a try. But, this doesn't solve where Amber is. I don't think Walling was our killer. At least we stopped him," Doyle said. "Then we've done good here. But, it doesn't solve who our killer is. I'll give Oscar a list of all the men I can remember, both here and in Detroit. Nothing says he couldn't have followed me from the city."

"I can check to see if there have been any new property sales or rentals to men from downstate. It may help," Mike said and went off to help his men.

Doyle stood there, and for the first time in a long time, he was at a loss for words. Amber was out there somewhere with this killer who taunts him. They had nothing to go on, no evidence or leads, to find his hideout.

Oscar came up behind Doyle, "Art, they're finished here except for the cadaver dogs. The State Police just arrived with them. How could Walling have done this if he had a tether on?"

"Back when we arrested Walling for pretty much the same thing he was doing here, he was very good with electronics. He probably rewired the tether so he could go out when he wanted. That's why I wanted to check the basement. It was where he murdered the others in the past. He just couldn't break out of his mold."

"Well, we need to get our minds back on our problem. If you can give me another list of men, I'll see what I can find. This one hit paid off, Walling won't be murdering anyone else."

"No, he won't. And good riddance to him. Okay, let's go back to your computer and see what other murderers and cutthroats we can find." Doyle yelled to Mike that they were leaving to go back to the station. Mike waved them off as he organized the State Police and their cadaver dogs to hunt for more bodies.

Doyle and Oscar went back to the Charger and drove out. They got back to the station, went in and over to Oscar's computer. He logged back into the database, as Doyle wrote out as many names as he could remember for men he put away. They spent the next hour writing out information about the men on Doyle's list. Nothing really hit for any of them being in the area in the last month. Most were still incarcerated in prison, or dead. There were two names that finally came up and showed promise.

"I remember this punk. I was in the FBI when the case was handed to us. He was a serial killer downriver in Detroit. Kept women for a week, torturing them, before killing and disposing of them in shallow graves on his mother's property."

"Ah, nothing more says I love you, Mom, like a dead body," Oscar laughed.

"Yeah, and he almost got off because his lawyer made a fuss over the search for the bodies on his mother's property. Luckily, the judge didn't like the lawyer and brushed him off. The case went to jury and they gave him life. Now he's being paroled after twenty years. Amazing, a conviction of life for multiple murders and they parole him for finding God. This is a sick world."

"Well, he's now in Detroit, but his parole officer reported he was moving out here to Oxford for work. I'd say he's a good candidate," Oscar said. "Strange that he comes to Oxford to work."

"Yeah, does it give a current address?"

"Yep, I wrote it down, a house he told his parole officer that he was renting," Oscar said and handed the paper to Doyle. "This other convict was released three weeks ago and his whereabouts are unknown. I dug further and he got a new driver's license that shows an address out by Hadley. Another coincidence?"

Doyle looked at the paper Oscar handed him and saw the address for the second man. "Well, we have some investigating to do, don't we?"

"I'm right behind you," Oscar replied.

"I know about where this first address is," Doyle said as they were driving out. "It's in a neighborhood where a guy I knew lived. I hope it's not the same house."

"Who's the second name?" Oscar asked.

"He was a lowlife junkie who murdered people for quick cash. He wasn't really a serial killer, but his motives were similar. Murder for cash. He attacked the wrong person one night, me. I was undercover hoping to pull him out and it worked. We were just lucky."

"Did you beat him within an inch of his life?" Oscar asked, grinning.

"I couldn't, there were too many other cops with me, all hiding undercover. I did get a punch in on his ugly face, though. Delbert Quinn was his name, I remember it well. I had to go to court to testify that he attacked me, and about the souvenirs he had taken from his other victims - wallets and purses that we found in his apartment. He didn't like me after that, even threatened me after he got a life sentence. Murder on four counts. I'm not happy they let him out, also."

"Well, maybe he's still in the murder business and we will stop him, too. And, hopefully find Amber in the process."

*

Chapter 13

They headed to the first name on the list, Joseph Larabee. Doyle said, "He's now too far from his mother's property to bury any bodies. Besides, I don't think after twenty years his mother is still alive. She was pretty old back then. This guy is no lightweight, and I'm sure he pumped up in prison. So be alert."

"Me and my .38 are always ready," Oscar replied.

They drove out a long dirt road and found the house. It was once part of a farm, but the barn was half gone. The boards probably sold to people to use in their homes. Barn wood was premium for remodeling projects these days. Doyle looked down the road to the house where his former friend lived, wondering what happened to him.

Doyle and Oscar went to the house and Doyle knocked on the front door. After a few moments, a woman answered the door. She was halfway attractive in a plain sort of way and had to be in her early thirties. About twenty years younger than Larabee.

"May I help you?" she asked.

"Is Joe Larabee in?" Doyle asked.

"He's at work right now. Is there something I can help you with?"

Doyle brought out his badge wallet with the private investigator badge that Val bought him. He flashed it and hoped she didn't get a good look at it, figuring he was a cop. "We just need to ask him a couple questions. Maybe you can tell us where he works and what his hours are?"

"He works at the State Park campground, he's a grounds keeper. He works every day from morning until about six. Is he in trouble?"

"No, you know for a fact he works there?"

"Well, he gets a paycheck from them, so I hope he's working."

"Are you his wife?" Doyle asked.

"Oh God, no. I wouldn't marry him. I just share the house with him. It was my family home and I needed money to keep it from being foreclosed on for back taxes. Joe helps with the payments and utilities. That's all."

"You've answered our questions, we're sorry to bother you. Thanks," Doyle said and they went off the porch.

She yelled, "Want me to give him a message?"

"No, that's alright." Doyle didn't need to start Larabee on the warpath if he knew Doyle had visited.

They got in the car and Doyle looked to the next address. He pulled out of the drive and went past the house where the guy he knew from his youth lived. He saw an old red van in the drive and the shades were all drawn in the house. He was trying to remember the name of the man, but he could only think of Skeeter. It was given to him because the man, or a boy back then, had a long pointy nose, like a mosquito. So he got the nickname Skeeter. But he couldn't remember his real name. It seemed like Bill, but it would come to him eventually.

They drove out from Oxford and up to the Hadley area. It wasn't much of a town, it was in the southwest corner of Lapeer County and had not much more than a post office, blacksmith, antique store, and ice cream and pizza parlor. They found the road that Delbert Quinn lived on and went to the building.

"This doesn't look like a killer lives here," Oscar said.

"This is the house of Delbert's parents. I'm sure they would take care of the place. But not their son. Shall we attack the castle?"

"Onward, Sir Losealot," Oscar said and got out.

They went to the door and knocked. After a few minutes, an older woman answered.

"Mrs. Quinn, is Delbert home?"

The woman looked distressed and said, "No, he's not here right now. What is this about?"

"I'm sorry ma'am. We're investigators and we need to know if your son is working?"

"His parole officer usually comes around to ask that. Yes, he's working as far as I know. He works at the local nursery down the road towards Oxford. I sometimes have to call him there and he answers."

Doyle thought that with a cell phone, he could answer from anywhere. Not necessarily at his work. "Is he there now?"

"As far as I know he is. Do you want me to call?"

"No, please, we'll just go there and talk to him. It's alright, ma'am, we just have a few questions to ask."

"You're that Detective Doyle who arrested my son, aren't you?"

Doyle was surprised that the woman recognized him. "I am, ma'am. I don't regret doing it, he murdered four people and I'm surprised they let him out."

"Detective, I'm not happy that my son committed those murders, but he is my son."

"Mrs. Quinn, I'm not a detective anymore. I'm a private investigator and we're trying to track down a murderer who is killing people in the area. Can you vouch for your son over the last few days?"

"When he isn't working, he's in his room playing on his computer. I know he's here because I insist he leave his door open. I don't tolerate any more murderous activity. And he knows it."

"Well, you answered our questions. Don't mention that I was here, it may upset Delbert."

"I'm not going to say a word that you were here. Now, if you could leave," she said tersely.

Doyle said nothing to upset the woman further and turned off the porch. Oscar was standing on the sidewalk and followed Doyle to his car.

"This is not going well. We have nothing so far. Any more men you put away?" Oscar asked.

"I gave all that I could think of. It's beyond me now. Damn, I hope Amber is all right."

"So far, the killer hasn't left any notes, so maybe he's not going to harm her," Oscar said.

"We haven't been back to the cabin all day. I'm afraid to go there and find another body. Especially Amber's."

"We have nothing else to track down. Take me back to get my car and laptop and we'll go to the cabin. Probably should have put a deputy on the place."

"I'll talk to Mike about that. If they're watching the cabin, the killer may have his plan disrupted."

Doyle's Justice

They arrived at the station and Doyle waited while Oscar went to get his laptop and then went to his car. They drove out and back to the cabin. Doyle pulled up and parked. He was nervous about going to the front porch.

Oscar came up behind him, "May as well go see," he said.

They went around and approached the porch. They found nothing.

"Damn, I'm getting frustrated. This guy is playing with my head, between killing people I knew and taking Amber, he's not gaining points with me."

"At least, maybe, she's still alive," Oscar said to help Doyle relax.

"I'll give him that, but he's toying with me. What the hell did I do to him that was so bad?"

"Doyle, you have to admit you're not a very nice person when it comes to criminals."

"Hey, I'm a sweetheart. Don't say that."

"I won't, but you know it's true," Oscar said.

"Just leave me alone, please," Doyle begged. He was getting frustrated and Oscar was now starting to sense it.

Doyle's cell phone rang out the *Jaws* theme and he looked at the caller ID, it was Mike. "Hey Mike, what's up?"

"We found Amber," Mike said into Doyle's ear, he put the phone on speaker and said, "Talk to me."

"A tourist was driving up Baldwin Road and spotted a body on the side of the road. He stopped and called 911, so we investigated. It was Amber.

She was alive, barely. They took her to the Oxford Pregnancy Center for treatment."

"Pregnancy? Why there?" Doyle asked.

"They have doctors and the nearest hospital is Havenwyck Hospital in Auburn Hills. We thought she needed immediate treatment and didn't want to risk transporting her. So she's being treated here for now, and when she's stable, they'll take her to Auburn Hills."

"Okay, thanks, I'll see you soon." Doyle disconnected and told Oscar to follow. They got in the Charger and drove out. "Can you find out where Oxford Pregnancy Center is on your phone?"

"Pregnancy? Why is she there?"

"Don't ask, just find it. I'm driving blind here."

Oscar checked the Google search on his phone and found the address and the directions. They got there shortly after. They parked and Doyle saw a couple sheriff's cars parked out front. They went in and Doyle showed his badge and asked, "They brought in a woman found on the road, for treatment. Where is she?"

The receptionist looked surprised as a doctor came up behind her and said, "She's being treated by our staff doctor now. If you'll go through that door, there are sheriff's men waiting."

Doyle thanked her and went to the door. He went into a waiting room and saw Mike with two deputies. "Mike, what happened?"

"Don't know yet, she was unconscious when they found her. We're waiting to see if she'll be all right. May as well wait with us."

They all sat in the waiting room for word on her condition. "Who found her?" Doyle asked.

"Some tourist from the campground. He was picking up food for the night and saw her lying on the side of the road. He stopped and found her still alive, he called 911. I got the call after the ambulance brought her here. Then I called you as soon as I found out she was still alive."

"Thanks for that. I'm not going to let her get captured again," Doyle said. "We need to put a detail on her now."

*

Chapter 14

"I'll get someone to watch her. She was really banged up with scrapes and scuff marks from what looked like being dragged on the road. Or, maybe she jumped out of a vehicle and rolled on the ground to the side. We'll find out when she awakens."

Mike, Oscar and Doyle sat waiting, finally a doctor came in. Doyle jumped up and went to him. "How is she, Doc?" he asked.

"She's all right, sleeping now from the sedative we gave her. She had a few bruises and scrapes on her face and arms, from what looked like moving across the ground. She may have been thrown from a car. I'll let you know when you can talk to her. We'll have to move her to a regular hospital, we're not set up here for her injuries. We typically only treat infants and new mothers, we only took her in because the situation was dire. She's stable enough to move now," he said with a smile.

"Well, we can breathe easy again," Oscar said.

"Yeah, but I still want this creep," Doyle said quietly.

About an hour later, a nurse came out and said Amber was awake and talking. The men went into the room where she was reclining on the bed. She gave a slight smile when she saw Doyle. Her face was bandaged up and she had a black eye.

Doyle went to her and said, "If you can talk, tell us what happened."

"I feel fine, thank you. I'm just hurting from my fall from the van. After you and Oscar left us, I went to the car to get a pack of cigarettes for Marie," she paused. "Is Marie all right?"

Doyle hated to tell her, "She's…dead."

Amber's face contorted and she started to tear up. Doyle grabbed a tissue from the box on a side table and gave it to her. She dabbed her eyes and said, "I had a horrible feeling that had happen. While I was out by the car, someone came up behind me and put what I assumed was a gun in my back. It was a man, and he said to stand still. He threw a bag over my head, tied it and turned me around. He grabbed my wrists and put tape on them to hold them together. Then he pushed me back to the cabin, I fell a couple times and he pulled me up. He was strong. Can I have a drink of water?"

Doyle's Justice

Doyle saw the cup with a straw, smelled it to make sure it was water and gave it to her. Amber's arms were bandaged also, covering her scrapes. She took a couple sips and handed the cup back to Doyle.

"We were in the cabin and I didn't hear Marie. He sat me on the bed and did something, I couldn't see. Then I heard dragging and the door opened. He went out."

"Probably when he took Marie out to the porch," Doyle said.

"He came back to me and took me out to where the cars were. I heard a door slide, like a van side door, and then he pushed me in. He closed the door and then drove off. I tried to remember the directions he was going, but he was driving around so much I got lost. Finally, he pulled down a dirt road, I could tell by the sounds. He came to a turn and a stop, then the side door opened again. He pulled me out and took me to a building. I could tell when he pushed me against the wall, then he opened an old screen door. You know that sound the spring makes on an old screen door, like that. He moved me in and told me to reach out." She pointed to the water again that Doyle was holding, held it up to her lips and she sipped.

"I reached out and he guided my hands to what felt like a stair railing. He said to follow it down to the basement and he'd be right back. I held the rail as I carefully stepped down. I got to the bottom and just stood there. I couldn't see what there was down there and didn't want to hurt myself."

Doyle looked to Mike and said, "He drives a van and it sounds like he has an older house on a dirt road. That will help."

Mike nodded. Then he asked, "Did you smell anything, Amber?"

She was thinking. "Yeah, there was a smell of fuel oil, like maybe he heated with it."

Mike said, "I can check with local heating oil companies to get a list of home customers. It will help to find him."

"You better move fast," Amber said. "I could hear him in the heating ducts, he was talking to someone, possibly on a phone, and saying that he was coming to visit for a few days, just to disappear with his trophy. I presume he meant me."

"How did you end up on the side of the road?" Doyle asked.

"I was in the basement for what seemed like forever, he was doing something upstairs, making noises. Finally, I could hear his footsteps coming to the stairs. He yelled down to me to find my way up. Then it sounded like he went outside. I found the handrail again and came upstairs. I waited at the top until he came in and pulled me outside. He pushed me in the van again and closed the door. I was trying to get the bag off my head, he had tied it at the back and I couldn't reach it with my hands taped in front. I was tugging at the string around my neck and it was finally giving way. I did manage to get the bag a little looser and pulled it up. Then, I could see. The van was dirty, there was a big tool box and a couple tires piled up in back. The one side of the van had shelves built in with boxes strapped in place. It looked like a work van. I turned to see if I could see the man, but there was a wall separating the front from the back. So I couldn't see him. But, he also couldn't see me. He started driving away as I crawled to the back doors and managed to open one side. I could see the road flying below us, and it was a choice to jump or stay with him. I chose to jump. That was the last I remember until I woke here. I do remember hitting the ground and the pain as I rolled across the pavement. Then I blacked out."

"Brave girl," Mike said, "and good thinking. I'll have a BOLO out for any vans on the roads going out of the area." He went out as Doyle leaned over and kissed Amber on the cheek, one that wasn't covered in bandages.

She smiled and said, "I thought of you most of the time I was kidnapped. I knew you'd try to find me."

"We did our best, but luckily you did our job for us. Is there anything else you can remember about the man?"

"He had a slight lisp, it was prominent when he talked with words having an 's' in them. His voice was fairly deep, not high, and he had to be strong, the way he lifted me up. Otherwise, I never saw him."

"Well, he's gone for now and you're safe. Did you hear anything on his phone call about where he might be going?"

"He didn't talk long, but I did hear him say something about a place where tigers used to play. Was he talking about a zoo?"

Doyle straightened up and turned to Oscar sitting behind him. "Call Marge and tell her to get away from the office and stay away until we get there."

Oscar stood, taking out his cell phone. He left the room to make the call. Doyle turned back to Amber.

"You're sure he said tigers?" he asked.

"I'm sure, he said they moved the tigers and he was going to where they were originally at. I thought it was odd that he would be interested in tigers."

"I think he was talking about the Detroit Tigers baseball team. Their old stadium is right around the corner from my office. It was torn down years ago and they moved the team to a new stadium. I think he's going to my office, but why? If I'm up here, what does he want down there?"

Amber said quietly, "Maybe he was going to kill me and put me in your office. He already dumped bodies at your cabin, so it would make sense that he could continue at your place of work."

"That really does make sense, but he's not going to be happy when he finds you're gone."

Oscar came back in and said, "I talked to Marge and she's leaving now. I told her we'd call when we knew more."

"Good, now we don't have to worry about her." He looked back to Amber, "I have to leave, are you going to be alright?"

"If you think he's going to your office, then you have to go there. I'll be here when you return, don't worry about me," she said.

"I'll be sure that Mike puts a guard or two on you, just in case. I should be back soon, I hope." He stood and took Oscar out with him.

"You really think this dipwad is going to our office?" Oscar asked.

"Well, he said he had Amber as his trophy and he said he was going to where the tigers used to play, I'd say it's a good bet."

*

Chapter 15

Outside the clinic, Oscar said, "What might happen if this guy finds Amber gone? Do you think he may turn around and come back?"

"Amber said there was a partition between the front of the van and the back. If this guy is heading down to Detroit, he may not know she's gone yet. Unless he stops at a rest stop, but for such a short trip, I doubt he would bother. I think he'll have a rude awakening when he gets to his destination."

"Well, it makes sense to harass you from the office also. But that implies that he's following you and knows what you're doing."

"True, but it's not like I'm hiding what I do. He could have talked to anyone in Oxford that I came in contact with and they could have told him about my business. All he'd have to do is look up the address of the office and go there. Amber said he was talking to someone, so he may have a partner in his crimes." Doyle turned as Mike came over from making his phone calls.

"So, what's happening?" Mike asked. Doyle explained what they found out from Amber and they were going back south. "I'll put a couple of my deputies in shifts on her, until I hear that you caught the bastard."

"That's good, I don't know if he'll come back for her when he finds she's missing, or if he'll find someone down there to kill," Doyle said.

"You should warn all your friends," Mike said.

"All my friends are cops, and I'm not real friendly with most of them. Oscar and Marge are the two closest to me right now, and we warned Marge to get away from the office. So that leaves Oscar." Doyle smiled and continued, "I could put Oscar out for bait."

"No, you're not, I'm not being bait for anyone. Use Marge for bait, she has her .357 magnum to protect her."

Doyle laughed and then said, "I'm not really sure if we have the right information. He may be going to my office, but when he finds Amber missing, it could change his plans. Mike, take all the info that we got from Amber and let's see if we can find his house here first."

"I'll call the heating oil companies and see if they deliver to an old house on a dirt road. That could be any number of places, but it's a start. Let's go back to the station."

Doyle's Justice

Twenty minutes later, they were making calls to the two oil companies that supply heating oil to homes. "There's only three that still use fuel oil to heat their homes in this area, and two are on a major road, asphalt. There's only one on a dirt road, and the customer's name is William Blain."

Doyle suddenly remembered the name, "Skeeter!" he shouted, just about causing Oscar to fall back in his chair.

"Where's a skeeter? It's too cold for mosquitos," Oscar said, righting his chair.

"No, the guy I knew from out in that house by Larabee. When we passed it, I saw he had a van, a red one in the drive. Damn, we were so close to Amber. He used to be called Skeeter."

"I know just who you're talking about," Mike said. "He used to be tormented because of his nose. If he thought you started that nickname, he might be lashing back."

"I didn't start the name. It was Gloria, the girl I was going with at the time, she named him that. He may have thought I did it. Gloria Waschevski, do you know her, Mike?"

"Yeah, she disappeared about a year ago, her husband was suspected of doing her in, but he had an iron clad alibi. He was out of the state for a week on business. We never found her. You think Skeeter did her in?"

"She did torment the hell out of him. She was a mean girl, which is why we broke up. If anyone needed doing in, it would be her. Let's go back to that house and see what we have."

They went out to their cars and drove to the property. Doyle pointed to the house down the road, the one Larabee was in, and said, "There's a serial killer ex-con living there. Just so you know."

"I'll keep that in mind. Thanks," Mike said. "Okay, I don't have a warrant, so you'll have to lead the charge again."

They noticed that the van was gone. Doyle went to the side door and opened the wooden screen door. The spring on the door made that noise they make, that Amber heard. Doyle tried the door but it was locked. "Mike, look away," Doyle said and put his elbow into the window. He cleared away the broken glass and said, "Hey, it looks like someone broke in, we may need to investigate. How's that for probable cause?"

Mike laughed and said, "I may need you around to help once in a while." Doyle opened the door and in front of him was the stairs to the basement that Amber described. "Since she was never up stairs, we'll start in the basement." They went down and could smell the fuel oil. "So far so good. Let's see what Skeeter has going upstairs." They went back up and into the house. It was a mess, like someone hadn't cleaned in a couple months.

Doyle was nosing around a desk that had papers scattered over it. He found a phone book for Detroit on top and it was opened to the section for Private Investigators. Doyle knew they weren't in the book yet, until it came out in the spring next year. He figured that Skeeter looked it up, and not finding it, probably called information. He found a pad of paper, and taking a pencil, he rubbed the lead onto the pad and brought up an address. Oscar was watching what Doyle was doing and he said, "That's our address at the office."

"It sure is and we now know he has plans to go there." Doyle turned to Mike and said, "This confirms his intentions of going there, so I think we need to leave. I hope we don't find a body in my desk chair."

"I'll have the forensic people go over this place to see if he had anything to do with Gloria's disappearance. May as well cover all bases."

"Good idea. I'll let you know what we find at our office. Keep an eye on Amber," Doyle said.

"I will. Be careful, and send his body back to me for burial." Mike smiled as they went out of the house.

"Are you going to say goodbye to Amber?" Oscar asked as they drove out from the property.

"No, I told her what was happening. I'm taking you back to get your car and we'll meet back at the office."

Doyle dropped Oscar off and headed over to Lapeer Road to drive south. About an hour later, he arrived at his building. He looked around the parking area for a red van and saw none. He got out of his car and went to the back door. He checked it to see if it was broken into. It wasn't. He put the key in and opened the door. He carefully went in with his Sig .9 drawn out front. The building was quiet, Marge had left, so the radio was off. He went up and checked around the partition walls he had installed around his desk and Oscar's. He saw no one. He spun around when the back door opened and aimed at the person entering.

"Hey, don't shoot. It's me," Oscar said. "A little jumpy are we?"

"I wasn't sure if he was here, but there are no bodies in the building." They went up to Marge's desk and looked out the front window to Michigan Avenue. There were no red vans parked around the area, so they relaxed.

"I guess we don't have much to do but wait for Skeeter's next move. I wish I could find a number for him, so I could call to taunt him," Doyle said.

"What did Mike say was his real name?" Oscar asked.

"William Blain, why?"

"Give me a minute. He went to his desk as Doyle came up and looked over the new wall. Oscar was dialing a number then waited. "Sammy, this is Oscar, can you do me a favor?" He listened then said "I need a phone number for a William Blain from the Oxford area code. Probably a cell phone if you can track that?" He listened again and then said, "Thanks Sam, call me if you get a hit," he gave the man his number and hung up.

Oscar stood and went around the wall to Doyle. "Maybe we'll get lucky. My friend is a wiz with phone numbers."

"You have hacker friends? More things I didn't know about you," Doyle said with a laugh.

"I've said it before, I'm a loveable person. I know a lot of the right people."

Doyle went back to the front window. "Maybe if we stand here long enough, Skeeter will see us."

"I hope he doesn't have a sniper rifle. I'd think twice about standing here," Oscar said, moving away from the window. Doyle looked back to him and then followed. No sense in tempting fate. "Hey, we've had a long day, let go home and get some sleep and meet back here in the morning."

Oscar agreed and they got ready to leave.

Across the street from their office, in the parking lot behind St. Peter's Episcopal Church, but in sight of the office, sat a red van. The man sat at the wheel, mad about losing his catch somewhere along the long drive down from Oxford. He'd have to regroup on his plan now. What could he do now to piss off Doyle? It was going to be a challenge.

*

Chapter 16

Doyle and Oscar arrived back at the office by eight o'clock the next morning and went in. It was quiet in the building and Doyle went to pick up the mail.

Doyle and Oscar were standing by the partition walls around Doyle's desk talking when they heard a noise at the back door. Both men pulled their weapons and waited. The door opened and Doyle yelled, "Freeze," scaring the crap out of Marge.

"What are you doing back here, we told you to stay away," Doyle said, holstering his weapon.

"I'm sorry, I saw your cars in the back and I have my gun, so I figured it was safe to come in. I rushed out of here when Oscar called, and forgot my knitting bag."

Doyle said, "You stay right there. Oscar, go get her bag." Oscar nodded and went up front and found the bag on the floor next to her desk.

"You really shouldn't have come back. We have a killer watching me and I don't want you to be hurt."

"I appreciate that, but I'd have nothing to do at home without my knitting," she replied.

"Okay, but Oscar is going to escort you to your car," Doyle said, then told Oscar to watch for any red vans. He said he would and took Marge out.

Doyle stood waiting for Oscar to return when the office phone rang. He answered, "Doyle Investigations."

"Can I talk to Oscar?" came a voice.

"He stepped out for a moment, I'm his associate, may I help you?"

"Yeah, I got the phone number for the name he gave me, and it's a cell phone, but I couldn't get any information about the owner. Although, I did check GPS location on the phone and it's working. The phone, right now, is at the south-east corner of Michigan and Trumbull. I hope that helps."

"It does, give me the number." Doyle wrote it down and said, "Thanks." Doyle was feeling numb, and hung up. He went off the side of the room to look out across the street at St. Peter's Episcopal Church on the corner across from the office. He scanned the area and then saw in the side parking lot towards the back, behind a dumpster, a red van. "Come on Oscar, get back in here," he mumbled to himself.

He heard the door open and close, then Oscar came up. "I didn't see anyone suspicious. Whatcha looking at?"

"Skeeter, he's across the street. Your buddy called about the phone number and said he had GPS tracking on Skeeter's phone. He's across the street behind that dumpster. See the top of the van, it's red."

Oscar went to his desk and got out his binoculars and trained them on the area. "Yep, it's a red van and someone is in it. What shall we do?"

"He's in front so he can't see what we're doing in back. Let's get to my car and drive around to box him in."

"Sounds like plan B. Let's go," Oscar said, and they headed to the back door. Doyle had his car running as Oscar got in. He drove out the alley behind the building and came out onto Trumbull. He turned left and held back until the light was green for him, then he peeled out and across Michigan to the entrance to the parking lot behind the church. He drove quickly and got to the dumpster, but the van was gone.

"Damn, how could he have known we were coming!" Doyle yelled, pounding on the steering wheel. "He had to move quickly, we didn't take that long getting here." Doyle was pulling up to the dumpster when he saw a paper stuck to the side. In big letters across the top he saw his name. He got out and went to the paper and pulled it away. It had been stuck up with duct tape. He read it and took it back to Oscar.

He sat in the seat and read, "*Doyle, you may have home court advantage, but I've got the ball in my court. Let's play.*"

"Damn him!" Doyle growled. "How did he know? Oscar, call your friend back and see if he has a fix on Skeeter's location now."

Oscar pulled out his cell phone and placed the call. "Sammy, Oscar here, thanks for the info, but can you give me a fix on the location of the phone now?" He sat listening, then, "Uh-huh…uh-huh, okay that's not good, but thanks." Oscar hung up.

"What? Where is he?"

"Sam tried to get a fix on the phone, but said right after he talked to you, the signal disappeared. Sam said even if the phone was shut off the GPS would still track, so Sam figures the battery had to be pulled to shut the phone down totally."

"This is not good. He's somehow out-guessing us. How could he know I talked to your friend and how did he know we were coming after him?" Doyle sat and thought. "I have an idea," he said and pulled the car away from the dumpster, driving back out of the parking lot. He got back to his lot and parked.

Doyle stood looking around the area, "Skeeter was talking on the phone to someone down here. There must have been someone watching us from the back." He turned and walked to the outside back wall of the office. He went to the phone box attached to the building and saw it was closed but not latched. He pulled the door open and saw it. A wireless bug.

"Damn, he bugged us. He knew about the call and how I knew he was across the street. But, he still couldn't know we would go after him without being warned." Doyle closed the phone box door.

"Aren't you going to remove the bug?" Oscar asked.

"No, he doesn't know we know, so we can use it to our advantage later. All office calls we make will be on our cell phones," Doyle said, and looked around again. He couldn't see anyone sitting in a car watching. "Skeeter took off, so his accomplice must have left, too. Now we have to worry about two people."

Doyle went to unlock the back door and they went in. "Now what?" Oscar asked.

"You tell me, as he wrote on his note, he has the ball in his court. We just have to be alert and wait. Give Marge a call to be sure she got home safely," Doyle said.

Oscar pulled his cell phone and called Marge. After three rings she answered. "Hey, Arthur, I was going to call you about your green scarf. Do you want your name on it?"

"Marge, this is Oscar."

"I know, Arthur, I'll do that and I'll have it when I get back tomorrow. Talk later." She hung up.

"Do you know where Marge lives?" Oscar asked Doyle.

"No, why?" Doyle asked.

"I think she's in trouble, she was calling me Arthur and asked about your green scarf, you wanted black. She's got to be in trouble," Oscar replied.

Doyle jumped up and went to a file cabinet and removed a manila folder. He pulled a sheet of paper from the file and said, "Let's go." They went out the back door.

"If that son-of-a-bitch is bothering Marge, I will kill him," Doyle said as he drove out.

They got to the street listed on Marge's application and parked down from the house. They got out and surveyed the area. It was a typical street with older homes all close together. No driveways, just parking on the street. They went around through a backyard about three houses down from where Marge lived. They suddenly jumped when they came face to face with a large Doberman. The chain wasn't long enough to get to them, so they went around the snapping animal.

They came up behind Marge's home and Doyle peeked through a window. He saw it was a bedroom he was looking at, but didn't see Marge. They went to another window and it looked into a kitchen. Doyle could see Marge through a doorway, sitting on a high back easy chair, looking distressed. He suddenly saw a man walk by the door. He didn't think it was Skeeter and he whispered to Oscar to go around the front door and knock. "When someone answers, say you are collecting for some charity. I'll see if I can slip in the back door."

Oscar nodded and went around the house. Doyle crept to the back door and carefully tried it. Luckily, it was unlocked. He slowly opened the door a crack so he could hear in the house. He heard Oscar knocking and then Doyle pushed the door open wider, going in. He moved through the kitchen and up to the opening to the living room. He listened as Marge went to the door. There was a big mirror on the opposite wall in the room and he could see the man standing against a wall behind Marge. It wasn't Skeeter.

He watched Marge open the door, and as soon as she did, Oscar said loudly, "Hi, I'm collecting to send wayward girls to summer camp, would you like to help the cause?" Doyle hoped Marge would understand what they were doing.

He saw the man raise his gun and move away from the wall. Doyle came around the corner, aimed and fired. He shot the man in the shoulder causing him to lose his weapon and drop to his knees. Marge jumped and turned. Oscar came in past her and had his gun out. Doyle moved forward and grabbed the gun from the floor and pulled the man up and threw him to the couch, holding his gun on him.

Marge was starting to weep, Oscar went to her and moved her to the chair she had been sitting in. She sat and said, "I thought I was a goner. He said he was waiting for his boss, then they would take care of me. I didn't ask what he meant, I didn't want to know. When you called, I told him if I didn't answer, someone would come looking to see if I was all right."

Doyle smiled and said, "You did good."

Chapter 17

"How did he find Marge?" Oscar asked.

"I presume the guy in back saw her come in and go out with you, so he figured they would have someone to take hostage. He probably followed her here," Doyle said.

"But if Skeeter disabled his phone, how did he know that this jerk had Marge. Marge said his boss was coming."

Doyle looked to the man, went to him and asked, "How are you talking to Skeeter?"

The man sat, not saying anything. Doyle looked to the wound in his shoulder, it was superficial, hardly any blood, but it was a wound. Doyle didn't want to kill the man, just have him talk. Doyle reached and grabbed the shoulder, squeezing it, until the man cried out.

"I'll keep doing this until you either talk or pass out. Then I'll revive you and do it again." Doyle squeezed again and the man yelled out.

"Okay! Bill has another phone that he uses to call me," the man said, half crying.

Doyle had always referred to the man as Skeeter, so hearing the name Bill threw him. "Where's your phone?" he demanded with another squeeze.

The man pulled his phone from his pocket and handed it to Doyle. "Did you give directions here to Bill, or Skeeter, as I call him?"

"Not yet, he said he'd call back."

Doyle turned to Oscar, "Go outside and look around to see if he's telling the truth. If he is, then Skeeter shouldn't be around." Oscar went out.

"Now, tell me what your boss has planned," Doyle said.

"I don't know now. He had a plan when he thought he had some woman from up in Oxford. She got away and he's not happy. He's trying to figure out what to do that will piss you off."

The cell phone in Doyle's hand buzzed. He looked at the tiny screen and saw it said Bill. Doyle smiled and answered it but didn't say anything. He listened after putting the phone on speaker.

"Cruse, do you have the woman?" a voice said.

"No, Cruse doesn't, but we have Cruse. So your gang is short a man," Doyle replied.

There was silence then the voice said, "Doyle, I'll take care of you and all your people. You can count on it."

"Go for it, Skeeter. You remember that name, don't you? I didn't give it to you, Gloria Waschevski did. But I'm sure you know where she is. The sheriff is going over your house searching for clues. They'll get you for her disappearance and the people who you murdered in the last week. I'll be there at your trial to watch them sentence you. Or, if you piss me off too much, I may shoot you and save everyone the hassle of convicting you."

"Screw you, Doyle," he said and hung up.

"I'd say I pissed him off," Doyle said with a grin. He put the phone in his pocket and pulled his own phone. He hit speed dial and waited. "Marco, I need another favor."

A half hour later, Marco Lupis, Doyle's detective friend who helped frame Val's ex-husband, showed up. "You only get three favors, and this would be number two. What is it now?"

Doyle pointed to Cruse. "He needs to be parked somewhere until I can get his boss. Can you lose him in the system?"

"The wheels of justice turn slowly. What's the story?" Marco asked.

"First, this is Marge, my receptionist, and the big guy is Oscar Drew, my partner in crime. Guys, this is Detective Marco Lupis, an old friend. Have a seat Marco and I'll give you the details."

Doyle spent the next half hour telling Marco about the last week. Marco sat shaking his head with every twist in the story. "This Skeeter is a nutjob. You say he was a friend?"

"I never claimed he was a friend. He was someone in school with me and I knew him. He was a nerd and didn't fit in with all of us cool people."

"You were never cool, and you still aren't. Did he say anything about what he's planning to do?"

"Nope, we had the sheriff up in Oxford investigating, so we'll need someone down here to make it official. Any idea who?" Doyle said with a smirk.

"I may consider that as your third favor," Marco said.

"I think it should be covered by the Cruse favor," Doyle said, looking at the perp on the couch. He was not happy and his wound was hurting and he said so.

"Think I should take him to a hospital?" Marco asked.

"Too much paperwork. Don't you have an unlicensed doctor in your pocket who can bandage him up?" Doyle asked.

"I may have one or two who work out of their garages. You don't need him right now, do you?"

Cruse was looking terrified. "Hey, I need a good doctor, not some med school dropout."

"Shut up, Cruse, a girl scout could bandage your wound." He turned to Marco, "How do you want to handle this?"

"So far, Skeeter hasn't committed a crime down here," Marco said. "I'd need to talk to your sheriff friend to start an investigation. I hate the rule that we can't do anything until a crime is committed. If your sheriff can push jurisdiction to me, then maybe I can do something. Skeeter will be a fugitive from Lapeer County."

"I'm not a cop anymore, so I don't have to follow rules," Doyle said.

"Just don't get caught," Marco grinned. "You know I'll look away, but be careful."

"Thanks, now you can haul this bum out of Marge's house so we can fumigate."

Marco stood and grabbed Cruse by the shirt and pulled him up. Cruse screamed out in pain. "I'm

110

sorry, did I hurt you?" Marco cuffed him, pulled him to the door and out. They could hear him yelling all the way to Marco's car.

"So, as far as we know, Skeeter doesn't know this address. So Marge should be safe, but I never go by safe theories. Marge, do you have a relative you can stay with for a few days?"

"Sure, my sister. She lives alone and I visit her from time to time. I could stay with her."

"Well, do that, just to be safe. Oscar, we need to find Skeeter."

"I'm open for suggestions," Oscar said.

"Hang on," Doyle said and ran out the front door. Marco was still out front putting Cruse in the car. "Hold on," Doyle yelled. "I need to ask him one question."

"Be my guest," Marco said.

Doyle leaned into the back of the car. Cruse looked frightened and said nothing.

"Cruse, you must have a hideout somewhere. Tell me where it is and I'll see you get first class medical attention." Doyle waited. Cruse said nothing. "Okay, dirty scalpels and thread stitches. Still won't help?"

Cruse stared at Doyle. "Bill will murder me if I give him up."

"We'll protect you. I want Skeeter, or Bill, to go away for a long time, or end up dead."

"Dead is the only way he'll be stopped," he paused. "It's in a garage called Horst Repairs on the corner of Cass and Ledyard Street. There's a door at

111

the back that leads into the main clubhouse, separate from the garage."

"Thank you Cruse. Marco, find a decent doctor for him." Doyle winked at his friend and Marco asked if he needed back up to go there.

"I've got you on speed dial if I need the cavalry. Let me take a look first then I'll decide if I'll get you involved."

"Be careful, that area has hangouts that are being watched by the gang squad. Don't get arrested."

"I'll call you to bail me out. Is there someone in gang squad I can talk to about Skeeter's friends?"

"Sure, Dallas Franks, he's the man. At the 5-6 precinct. Tell him I sent you, but he may hit you. Maybe." Marco laughed and went around to the driver's side. "I'll keep you informed about Cruse."

"Thanks," Doyle said and went back to the house.

Marge had packed a couple of bags with clothes and her knitting. "Take a couple days off, I'll call if things change," Doyle told her.

"Thank you, Arthur. It will be good to catch up with her. I called and she's thrilled to have me visit." Oscar said he'd take her bags to her car and went out the back door to the alley where her car was parked.

Marge went out and Doyle said he'd lock up. She went to her car and got in, driving out. Doyle hoped she would be all right.

Doyle turned to lock the door then went around the building to his car. Oscar was following him and they went off. "Where's the 5-6?"

Oscar told him and gave him the directions. They arrived at the precinct and went in. The desk sergeant was friendly and asked them who they needed.

"Dallas Franks, if he's in?" Doyle said.

"I'll check," he said, then he made a call. "Dallas is in his office, gang squad in the back."

They thanked him and went into the building. Doyle had to ask where the office was at and they finally found it. A big man in gang colors asked what they wanted. Doyle figured he was an undercover cop and said, "Dallas Franks."

The man yelled in a gruff voice across the room, "Dallas, somebody to see you."

Doyle looked out across the cubicles, when he saw a head pop up. It had to be Dallas Franks.

*

Chapter 18

"Come on over," he yelled.

Doyle and Oscar walked around the desks and got to the cubicle of Dallas Franks. He gave them a smile and said, "You're Art Doyle, right? The cop who shot the mayor."

"Yes, unfortunately I am. I'm also getting tired of hearing it," Doyle replied.

"Enough said, now what can I do for you two?"

"I'm no longer a detective, I'm now private and this is my partner, Oscar Drew."

"Sure, I know of Oscar. You two are both well-known from the incident that I won't mention. Crazy Joe, who you shot in the head - good shot by the way - was one of the leaders of the gang we were following. You helped us to close that chapter. Thanks, now what do you need?"

"It's a long story, got some time?"

"Sure, sit and talk to me." Franks motioned to the chairs and they all sat. "Whatcha got?"

Doyle went over the last week to the man as Franks sat listening. Doyle was trying to be concise but accurate and told the whole gory story about Tammy, the insurance man and Marie. Then told of the kidnapping of Amber and how she escaped.

"Clever girl, is she all right?" Franks asked.

"She doing fine, last I heard." Doyle finally got to the part about Cruse. "So we caught this hood trying to kidnap our receptionist in her home, but we stopped him. He's presently in custody with Marco Lupis."

"Damn, you had to mention Marco, he owes me money from a bet we made."

"He said you might hit on us if we mentioned his name, but I'm not paying his debts."

"No worry, Doyle, I'll track him down one day. So, Cruse is actually Harvey Cruse, part of the Cass Street Gang. Bad people. What does your Skeeter have to do with them?"

"Well, Cruse insinuated that Skeeter, AKA William Blain, was his boss. We thought he might have some cred with this gang."

"Blain sounds familiar. You said he was from up by Oxford? Does he have a place down here?"

"Not that we know of. I'm hoping you might know."

"Hold on," he said and turned to his computer, typed in the name and waited. The screen changed a few times then an image came up. "Here's Skeeter Blain from the last time we arrested him two years ago, in a drug bust. He got off due to arresting officers not reading him his rights."

"Damn loopholes. They can take all the lawyers and put them on a boat to China," Doyle said, then thought about Gwen, his former girlfriend and a lawyer. "Maybe not all of them," he finished.

"I'll agree with you there. According to this, your buddy told us he lived in St. Clair Shores and was just visiting a friend at the house in question. A drug house. Some friends he has."

"Where in St. Clair Shores does it say he lived?" Doyle asked. "Can you print out that photo?"

Franks hit a button and printed out the photo, handing it to Doyle. "It doesn't say where he lived. They took his word he lived there, but he had no ID to put him in a residence. They wanted to hold him for vagrancy, but his lawyer cited his arrest as illegal. So he skated without further ado. Lucky bastard."

Doyle's phone rang out *Jaws* startling Franks. "Sorry, it's my ring tone," Doyle said as he pulled the phone out. He saw it was Mike Twain. "Hey, Mike. What's happening?" He put it on speaker.

"Doyle, you got some creepy friends. We had cadaver dogs brought back in to Skeeter's property and they found eight shallow graves with various decomposing bodies of women, according to Elwood. Elwood said he's had his limit of bodies, and he's blaming you. Have you found Skeeter yet?"

"No, we're slowly working towards it. I'm with the Detroit police gang squad leader and he's helping us."

"Gangs, is Skeeter part of a gang? I wouldn't think a serial killer would involve others in their kills."

"He wouldn't, but Skeeter needed help down here and he called a friend to help. He happens to be in a gang."

"Well, between the eight bodies we found, and the three of your acquaintances, I'd say he does fine on his own."

"For sure, keep me informed. Oh, did you find Gloria?"

"I got her husband tracking down her dentist to check her teeth against the bodies we found. One of them could be her."

"Too bad. Other than being mean, she wasn't a bad girlfriend. Let me know. How's Amber doing?"

"We've got her home and resting. I put two shifts on her to watch, but I don't think Skeeter will be back. Best to be safe than sorry."

"Tell her I miss her and we'll be up to visit when we get Skeeter."

"You got it, talk later." Mike hung up, so did Doyle.

He looked to Franks and said, "We now have a full blown serial killer. I'll call Marco and see what he can get started."

"I'll have my men digging into the Cass Street Gang. Maybe one or more of them is helping your friend."

"He's not my friend, and I'll put him in hell before he hurts another person," Doyle said.

"I'm sure most of our officers will look away when you do. Give me your card so I can call you."

Doyle handed Franks his card and they said their goodbyes. Doyle and Oscar left and went back to the car.

They sat in silence for a moment. "You're going to the gang's clubhouse, aren't you?" Oscar finally spoke.

"Well, Skeeter may be there, so we should go check it out."

"I don't want to end up as some hulking ape's bitch," Oscar said.

"You won't, I'll protect you," Doyle said.

"Who's going to keep you from becoming some ape's bitch?" Oscar grinned.

"You can be impossible, Oscar. We'll be careful, and besides, we're armed."

"So are they," Oscar said quietly to himself as Doyle drove out.

Doyle maneuvered through traffic and over to Cass Avenue. He drove until they found Horst's Repair and parked around the side. They got out and walked to the back while Oscar was watching for attacks from big hairy men in black leather.

They went to the back and saw there were four motorcycles parked behind the building, but no big hairy men. Doyle looked around wondering if Franks had men watching the building. He went to the door and opened it. The interior was dark, but he could see light further into the large building. It looked like a warehouse with a fairly high ceiling full of beams and hoists. Doyle wondered how many men had been hoisted up by their arms, just to be beat on.

They could hear loud voices in the lit area, so they went forward through the dark. Doyle glanced at the photo of Skeeter and handed it to Oscar, to familiarize himself with the man.

They came to the edge of the well-lit area and saw four men playing on a pool table. They hadn't seen Doyle and Oscar yet. Doyle stood watching them and didn't see Skeeter amongst them. One of the men glanced into the darkness and was startled. He came up with a pool cue and said, "Who are you?"

Doyle stood his ground and said, "Friends of Skeeter." He was hoping to get a reaction and he did.

"Screw Skeeter, you don't belong here." The four of them started walking toward Doyle. They stopped just outside the area of the light. Oscar was standing back in the dark of the room, with his gun drawn.

"You evidently don't like Skeeter. I don't either."

One man said, "You just said you were a friend, which is it?"

"Skeeter murdered three of my friends and I'm looking for him. I'm not happy about the murders."

The men laughed and one said, "Skeeter is a stone-cold killer. He's left bodies all around here in Detroit, before he ran back home up north. He had to, he murdered one of our own. So we aren't happy with him either. We haven't seen him, or he'd be dead."

"Harvey Cruse has seen him," Doyle said.

"Cruse? That weasel. He can go to hell with Skeeter."

"Skeeter doesn't like being called Skeeter. Why do you call him that?"

"Because he doesn't like it. For a lowlife who comes around once a year, we can call him what we want."

"Do you know where he might be?"

"Whatcha going to do when you find him."

"I'm wanting to kill him, but that would be against the law," Doyle smiled.

"You a cop, you look like a cop?" the smallest of the men said.

"I was a cop," he tried a new tact. "I was the cop who shot Crazy Joe."

"Whoa!" the men all started to raise their voices. "You saved us a lot of problems, dude. We wanted Crazy Joe out of the picture for years. You did us a big favor. You're Doyle, right?"

"Glad to see everyone knows me. Yes, I am. Now, can you tell me anything about Skeeter?"

"Come on over and talk, man."

Doyle looked back and told Oscar to follow. He came out of the darkness as the men tensed seeing him. "He's alright, he helped me by shooting Crazy Joe's men."

They relaxed and then went back to just past the pool table where they had couches and chairs set up.

"Sit, Doyle, let us tell you about Skeeter."

*

Chapter 19

"What can we tell you about Skeeter? You got some time?" the biggest of the men asked. He had tattoos all up and down his arms and across his neck. "Skeeter was evil. He was friggin' evil. He came here the first time to see someone he knew. We took him in as a friend, but had no idea what he was up to. After a week, he murdered our leader, Tokyo, and tried to say it was self-defense. Little Aaron told us that he saw Skeeter come up close to Tokyo and when Tokyo turned away, Skeet threw a wire around his neck and just about cut his head off. Self-defense, bullshit."

Another man, young, black and looked like he had an eating disorder or AIDS, piped up. "We confronted Skeeter and he pulled a gun, then he took off. We haven't seen him since and don't want to.

You kill him and you're a life member of the Cass Street Boys."

Another man spoke up, "Our connections in a few other friendly gangs said he tried to settle in with them, but they said all he wanted to do was murder people. We put out the word on him and then heard he left town. He had no cred here anymore. Why is he back, Doyle?"

"He's not happy with me for something that happened years ago. I'm not sure what sparked it recently, but he wants to make my life miserable. He dropped three bodies around my cabin in Metamora. Not all at once, but over three days. Then he came down here to mess with my office and I followed. So far, I don't know what he's up to down here."

"Man, if we hear anything, we can get hold of you," the black man said. Doyle handed him his card.

Doyle was about to thank him, when his phone rang. The four men jumped hearing the Jaws theme. "Sorry, it's my ring tone," Doyle said and looked at the caller ID, it said private.

"You don't have any sharks in your pockets, do you?" the big man asked. They all laughed.

"No, it smells up the suit," he replied and excused himself, answering his phone. "Doyle here?"

He listened then said, "We'll be right there." He hung up, looking to Oscar. "There's a dead body hanging on a light pole in front of our office. Sorry guys, love to chat more but I have to go ID a body. Crime doesn't stop."

Doyle stood, along with Oscar, they left the men. In the car, Doyle said, "I hope it's not someone I know, although I don't know many people around here. I'm sure Skeeter doesn't know anyone down here that I know."

They pulled up to the front of their office where the police had it cordoned off with the yellow tape. There were officers directing cars around the blockage on Michigan. Doyle got out and went to the tape. Marco was standing in the middle of the area and saw Doyle and Oscar. He waved to them to enter the scene.

They went over to Marco and saw the woman tied to the lamp pole in front of their office by her neck. She was wearing jogger's clothing and a headband. There was a small pack around her waist and a cord to ear buds hanging from the pack.

"So, clients hang themselves waiting for you to show up?" Marco said.

"You owe Dallas Franks for a bet," Doyle said.

"He'll have to find me. Take a look at the woman and tell me if you know her."

Doyle moved to the sidewalk and around the body to face the woman. He studied her face but nothing popped in his head. "Did you find any ID in her bag?"

Marco move up and read from his notepad. "Marisa Hollison, lives about two miles from here. She was jogging in the parking lot behind your building, which is the last place her watch showed."

"Watch?" Doyle asked.

"Yeah, she had one of those GPS jogger's watches that keeps track of her route and times. The thing stopped behind your building about an hour ago. Coroner says she's been dead about that long. I'm amazed no one has come forward after seeing your buddy hang her here."

"Quit calling him my buddy," Doyle said, feeling repulsed by the woman hanging there. He looked to Oscar and said, "We need security cameras installed here."

"I'll see what I can find to put up," Oscar said.

"A little late for that," Marco said.

"True, but Skeeter won't stop and I want him on camera. Just to see if he screws up." He turned to Oscar. "Go ahead and get some of those small cameras that we can watch on our phones. One or two for the front and the same for the back. Especially the back."

"I'll get it done," Oscar said and went over to open the door to the office and in.

They had to move back as the coroner and his men went to take the body down. They had the gurney beside her and then pulled her on to it. They flipped the black bag around her and zipped her in. What a terrible way to end up the last day of your life, in a black bag, Doyle thought.

"Skeeter is just striking out blindly now, since he has no idea who I know. He can hit on any one of seven hundred thousand people," Doyle said.

"That many?" Marco asked.

"Give or take a few thousand people. But it's now a hit or miss," Doyle said as he heard a ringing coming from his pocket. "Damn, I forgot I had Cruse's phone." He pulled it out and looked at the tiny screen. It said, Bill. "It's him," he said and answered. "You're not funny, Skeeter."

"What's the matter, Doyle, you didn't like my little present? She was fast and sleek, and just your speed. You move fast, and so did she. Now I need someone who is just as smart as you are. So watch your back." He hung up.

"He's leaving clues, I think. He said she was fast like me, now he's going after someone as smart."

"Smart in intelligence or smart mouthed? That would include my smart-assed ex-wife. I hope he tracks her down. Give me the phone and I'll see what our electronic people can find on it. Maybe it will give us a way to track him."

"Last time I tried that, he disabled his phone. Better hope he needs this phone," Doyle said as he handed the phone to Marco.

"Let's go in, I'd like to see a real live P.I. office. I may want to be a private investigator one day and need to know how to set up my office."

"Fine, follow me, and don't touch anything," Doyle laughed.

They went in and found Oscar on the phone. Doyle took Marco to his new cubicle and told him to sit.

"Damn, I didn't know you'd have a cubicle, I'd have guessed you'd go for the open-air concept in offices. Isn't this like your old office at the 4-6?"

Doyle looked around his cubicle and suddenly realized he was imitating his old office. He stood and asked Marco to help him. He pointed to the wall in front of his desk and said, "Start pulling on that, while I pull the side wall." They dragged the partitions around his desk and pulled it to the back. They set it up against the back wall.

"Now we have an interrogation room," Doyle said with a grin. They went back to his desk and sat.

"Is this better?" Marco asked.

"Much. I never liked being hemmed in."

Doyle had an epiphany, he was trying to imitate his old office with the walls. He looked around and breathed a big breath of air. "Yes, it's much better." He looked over to Oscar behind his walls and wondered if he wanted walls or not. Doyle didn't really ask him, so he'd leave it up to Oscar if he wanted to remove the walls.

"So, we now have an idea of who he may grab next. Someone smart," Doyle said.

"So, there's the Wayne State campus with plenty of scholars, or the government offices with all those self-proclaimed smart-ass officials. Take your pick."

"Let's see what your people can get off the phone," Doyle responded.

Oscar stood and came around his wall. He stopped when he saw Doyle's walls were gone. "Did you get robbed?" he asked. Doyle pointed to the back where Oscar saw the walls. "Can I take mine down, I really hate them, I feel like I'm back in the precinct."

Doyle stood, waved Marco over, and the three men pulled the walls away and joined them with the others, forming one big private room.

"Now you can put a bed back here to entertain your lady friends," Oscar mugged.

"I'm not looking for any lady friends until Skeeter is caught. What did you find out about the cameras?"

"I called my friend Sammy and he told me what to get. They have them at Walmart. Tiny cameras that work on batteries and send video to a transmitting device, then broadcast to our cell phones. They'll work off our Wi-Fi, too."

"Well, good thing we had Wi-Fi put in. So, why don't you run over and pick up the things and install them," Doyle said.

"I'd just put them in backward, Sammy said he'd come over to install them. I'll be back shortly."

Doyle turned to Marco and said, "Now to find out where smart people hang out."

*

Chapter 20

Doyle and Marco sat at Doyle's desk and talked. "So tell me about this Skeeter. You grew up with him?"

"Are you going to profile him?" Doyle asked.

"If you can fill in all the details. What makes Skeeter tick?"

Doyle sat back thinking about the man and how he came to be the evil criminal he is today. "I remember him as being Bill Blain, a quiet nerd who didn't bother anyone. He wanted to stay in the background and do his own thing. There were a number of boys in school who were privileged; you know the type, rich. They hated people below their station, and let them know they did. Bill wanted to be left alone, but they targeted him for their hate. I wasn't part of those boys, I didn't know any of them very well. I was going with a girl named Gloria, she was what they call a bitch. But she was sexy and kissed very well." Doyle laughed and got up. "Want something to drink? Our refrigerator is stocked with a couple types of liquids. Mostly bottled water and soda pop."

"Do you have Pepsi?" Marco asked.

"Yep, you and Oscar share a love for it." Doyle went to the fridge and took out a bottle of water and a Pepsi. He came back and sat.

"So, Bill became the joke du jour of the rich boys. He tried to ignore them, but it's hard to do when you are not as strong as your opponents. He was the proverbial ninety pound weakling. I felt like helping him when they would pick on him, but I was outnumbered myself."

"Wimp," Marco said.

Doyle ignored him and continued, "Finally, Gloria was bugged by Bill's prominent nose. It was fairly long and pointed. Gloria started calling him a human mosquito, which worked down to Skeeter. I knew he hated it, but again he couldn't do much. I broke up with Gloria shortly after, she was too mean for me."

"Wow, someone who's meaner than you. She must have been bad."

"And now she's most likely dead because of it. I'll know more when Mike calls me with his results from the dental exam." Doyle took a big swig of the bottled water and set it on the desk. "The name stuck with Skeeter and he had to endure it until he graduated from high school. I hated my high school, too many jerks and bitches."

"What happened to Skeeter after high school?"

"I heard that he went to work at his father's landscaping company. Something I never associated with Skeeter was that four of the boys who tormented him died in a tragic car accident shortly after graduation. I don't know if he had anything to do with it, but I'll have Mike look into it. I was moving on with my life and ended up going into the FBI in their Terrorist Task Force. I hadn't heard about Skeeter until just this week. Now I can't get him out of my life."

"Why is he taking it out on you with all these killings?"

"I'm not sure. I didn't give him the nickname, although he may have thought I did. Association with Gloria gave me a target on my back. Maybe he just loved the thrill of the hunt and kill, and I was handy. I won't know until we catch him."

"You think we will. A lot of serial killers just fade away, and disappear until they kill again years later. How many serial killers did the FBI catch while you were on the team?"

"I was with the terrorist finders, so we didn't worry about serial killers. When I first joined the Feds, I was assigned a few cases involving murders, so I got my feet wet that way. Terrorist kills were part of my mission. We enjoyed taking them out when we could find them."

"So you were a dangerous man?" Marco held his Pepsi up saluting him.

"I did what I had to do to save America from the dreaded infidels. Did you ever serve in the armed forces, you never said in all the time I've known you."

He grinned and said, "First Cavalry, Viet Nam. Helicopter door gunner most of the time. I saw a lot of the country from the air."

"Wow, I'm impressed. I avoided Nam by going into the FBI. They need us here to protect the country from the silent enemy."

"I'm not crazy about what I did. But I wasn't in the jungles having the crap scared out of me. I knew a few of the ground forces and they were basket cases. I hear that the troops in Iraq had it just as bad. Not knowing where the enemy was and how long you would last."

"Skeeter is out there hunting up his next victim, and we don't know who he's going to grab."

The front door opened and both men jumped up with their weapons drawn. They turned to the front where there stood a young-looking, skinny boy in a t-shirt with Einstein's E=MC2 printed on the front. He looked shocked at the sight of the guns, and said, "Is Oscar here?"

Doyle was laughing to himself, he figured it was Sammy, Oscar's friend. Doyle holstered his Sig and went to the boy. "Are you Sammy?"

He stood, looking nervous. "Yes, I am. Is Oscar here?"

"He went to get the surveillance cameras that you recommended. He should be back soon. Have a seat."

Sammy sat at Marge's desk and was looking out the window. "Did you know there's some guy out front across the street watching this office with binoculars?"

Doyle turned quickly as Marco came over. They were off to the side to hide from Skeeter. Doyle peeked around the window and saw a man in a car with binoculars. Suddenly, the man brought up a rifle through the side window and fired into the office. Sammy cried out and fell from his chair. Doyle ran to the broken window and started firing at the car parked across from the office. The car took off as Marco and Doyle ran out of the building and onto the street firing their guns at the departing car.

Doyle thought about Sammy and ran back into the building. He went to the boy and felt his pulse, it was still pumping. "Marco, call for a bus, now, he's still alive."

Marco pulled his phone and reported the shooting and requested an EMS. Doyle turned the boy over, as he was bleeding from his chest. He had some medical training and knew how to apply pressure to the wound. He did and hoped the EMS would get there soon.

They heard the back door open and Oscar yelled, "Lucy, I'm home." He came forward to see his friend on the floor, blood around him. "What the hell?"

Oscar yelled and came over. He knelt down and asked what happened.

Doyle quickly explained and Oscar went to the broken window looking out. "He's gone, Oscar. He shot your friend and drove off. We tried to fire on him, but he got away."

They could hear sirens in the distance coming closer. Doyle kept pressure on the wound as Oscar and Marco stood by watching. Oscar ran out of the building to signal the ambulance as to where they were.

Doyle looked to Oscar when the Medical team had the boy on a gurney and were taking him away. "Skeeter said he wanted someone smart. Sammy was smart, but how did Skeeter know?"

"Damn it, Doyle, Sammy was only nineteen years old. If he dies, I'm killing Skeeter myself.

*

Chapter 21

Doyle had called for an emergency glass company to come replace the window. Marco went off to take the cell phone to his electronic unit for exam and Oscar was sitting at his desk reading the instructions to put up the security cameras.

Doyle was watching around the front of the building for Skeeter. He didn't need any glass workers dead. The air was not the freshest today, but he took in a big breath. He stood on the sidewalk watching traffic carefully, not taking any chances and wanting to take a shot at Skeeter.

The supervisor of the glass workers came up and asked, "Did you know you have a vibration microphone on your window?"

Doyle quickly turned to the man and saw he was holding the small device that transmitted sounds made from a room through the glass. He reached over and took the bug from the man and thanked him. So that's how Skeeter could know what they were plotting. He had the phone bugged, now the office. He was wondering if Skeeter had worked in some kind of government dark ops to have all these toys. He studied the bug and pulled the battery out of it.

"If you see any more bugs, let me know," he said to the boss of the workers as they moved the new glass into place. He took the unit into the building and over to Oscar. "The glass people found this on the window. It transmits what we say by sound vibrations on the window. Like holding a drinking glass to a wall and listening to a conversation in another room. The son-of-a-bitch was listening to us as we spoke. That had to be how he knew Sammy was coming. He got his smart person."

"That's just putting another nail in his coffin. I want his scalp now," Oscar grumbled.

"Think you can put up the cameras without Sammy?"

"Actually, it's not that difficult, even for me. I just mount the cameras and press two buttons on the transmitting unit. The camera and base unit pair up and the signal goes through the Wi-Fi router and out to our phones. I'm going to mount one in the back facing the door and one aimed out to the parking lot. The one aimed at the door has motion sensors and will send us a notice telling us someone is at the door. They'll also record video so we'll have proof who was here. I'll put the other two on the front of the building, set up the same way. Both doors will be watched."

"Let me know when you are ready to install them and I'll help," Doyle offered.

"I'm about ready now. Shall we start with the back while the glass people are working?"

Oscar gathered the two tiny battery operated cameras and they went out to the back. After a half hour of setting up the cameras and adjusting them, they went to the front to start the next two. The glass people had finished and so they had the room to move now. They had all four cameras mounted and Oscar was showing Doyle how to access them from his Android cell phone.

"Just tap the thumbnail picture to see the camera you want to watch," Oscar explained.

Doyle tapped the picture of the back door and the image grew to show a live action video. "I like this. You say this is being recorded?"

"Only if there's movement at the door, then the camera will record the person. And, you'll get a notice that the camera was activated," Oscar said.

"Okay, we're now moving into the future, we need some more gadgets to help with surveillance."

"I'll go online and see what's available." Oscar sat at his desk and busied himself hunting for gadgets.

Doyle went to the front window and looked out. Doyle's cell phone sang its ominous tune and he saw it was Marco calling. "Hey, whatcha got?"

"Well, Skeeter must have figured you still had Cruse's phone because he called and asked to talk to you. I had my tech people run a quick trace on the phone, since they were already working on it. I told Skeeter you were out. He swore at me, and told me to tell you that since you were once a cop, he was going to go after someone in law enforcement next. Doyle, if he kills a cop, he's dead meat."

"Good, I won't cry over his funeral."

"I've got an APB and a BOLO out for him. I pulled his arrest records and sent the photo out. He's now wanted for the murder of the jogger and the shooting of a minor, and I added the murders of three people in Lapeer County. I also threw in that he threatened to murder a cop. That should stimulate some action."

"Did you get a hit on the trace of his conversation?" Doyle asked.

"No, he wasn't on the phone long enough, but he's in the area. Just couldn't pinpoint him. His phone isn't GPS capable, so we can't find him that way." Marco paused then said, "I was thinking, you should keep an eye on Oscar. He was once a cop and is your partner. Skeeter would just love to hit at you through him."

"First thing I thought when you told me he was going after a cop. I'll keep a good eye on him and stick like glue to him."

"Another thought, he knows you're friends with the sheriff up in your hometown, maybe give him a call to warn him."

"Good idea, Skeeter may go back home and start over there. Especially since he's on the wanted list here now. I'll call Mike when we finish. Thanks, and keep me informed." They finished and Doyle dialed Mike.

"I was beginning to worry that Skeeter got you," Mike said when he answered.

"No, but he's annoying me immensely." Doyle explained the situation and then told him about the threat to a cop.

"Well, if he comes back here, I'll have my men watch for him. Are you staying down there?"

"For a little longer. I want to come up and see how Amber is doing, but Skeeter comes first. How is Amber?"

"I saw her this morning and she's looking better. Her abrasions are healing and she's in good spirits. She said to say hi if I talked to you."

"Tell her I'll see her soon. Thanks, and be careful."

Mike said he would and hung up. Doyle looked to the front door as a man entered. Doyle was ready for anything now, and he heard Oscar get up from his desk. The man was in his late twenties and not very well dressed, plain shirt and jeans. Doyle felt he was a lowlife and possibly from some gang. He was ready for whatever the man could pull.

"May I help you?" Doyle asked.

The man seemed nervous and said, "I need some investigating to see if my wife is cheating."

Doyle didn't relax. He saw the man wasn't wearing a wedding band. "What's your wife's name?"

The question surprised him, like he didn't know her name. "Uh, it's…Linda."

Doyle moved to his desk and said, "Cheating? Why do you think this?"

"May I sit at your desk and explain?" the man asked.

Doyle hesitated, feeling the man wanted something. "Sure, come here and sit."

The man moved quickly and sat down on the client chair next to Doyle's desk. He had his arms down his sides and said, "My wife has been going out a lot. I think she's seeing someone."

Doyle was watching the man closely, something was off. Doyle watched the man in his peripheral vision while staring at his face. He could see the man subtly reach his hand under the chair.

"So, do you think your wife is fooling around with Skeeter Blain?" Doyle asked.

The man's eyes went big and he jumped up, but Oscar was behind him, now blocking the front door. Oscar threw out a punch at the man and he went down. "Damn, that felt good," Oscar said.

The man was rolling on the floor holding his chin. Doyle and Oscar pulled him up and Doyle zipcuffed him to the chair. Then Doyle reached under the chair and pulled out the tiny bug that the man was planting.

"You aren't very good at subversive operations. But then again, you are just a punk from Skeeter's boys. Oscar, call Marco and have him come get this scum." Doyle sat and leaned forward. "There will be a large, unruly cop coming to get you. I may see my way to being sure he doesn't hurt you if you help me out."

The man was nodding his head quickly, and said, "What do you want? I told Skeeter it was a dumb idea to come waltzing in here to plant the bug. He hit me and told me to do what he said. I left, I knew it wouldn't work."

"Okay, shut up and listen." Doyle held up the bug and said closely to it, "Skeeter isn't very bright. He's just a thug who can kill people through stupidity. He's going to get caught and will spend the rest of his life in prison or I'll see he dies. You hear that Skeeter?" Doyle looked at the man, closing his fist around the bug. "This thing is live, right?" The man nodded.

Doyle knew the range on the bug couldn't be very far. He started the app on his phone to look out at the front camera. He couldn't see anyone sitting openly in a car. That didn't mean he wasn't out there. "Where's Skeeter right now?" Doyle asked the man.

"He's on the side of the building." He said barely loud enough for Doyle to hear. Oscar was heading to the door when Doyle yelled to wait. Doyle took the bug and put it into a glass of water he had sitting on his desk. "It could be a trap, Oscar. To get us out in the open."

*

Chapter 22

"Why a trap?" Oscar asked.

"Think about it. Skeeter was clever enough to put a bug on our phone, then a bug on our window. Do you really think he'd send in this goofball to plant a bug in the office?" Doyle said.

"Okay, you got a point."

Doyle leaned to the man and said, "Did Skeeter tell you to get caught and then tell us he was around the side of the building?"

The man didn't speak. Doyle reached over and grabbed his nose and pulled. "Ow, man, that hurts," he said when Doyle let go.

"Good, then you know what pain feels like. How about I make that pain worse by taking you in our back room and beat the crap out of you?" Doyle pointed to the partition walls standing in the back. "It's our interrogation room, where we have ways to make you talk."

The man leaned forward to look at the walls then sat back. "Yeah, Skeeter was going to have me get caught and then draw you out."

Doyle smiled at Oscar and pulled his cell phone. He speed dialed Marco and explained what was going on. Marco said he'd have cars converge on the area. "What kind of car is it?" Marco asked.

Doyle asked the man, "What kind of car is Skeeter in?"

The man didn't say anything, then Oscar bumped his chair. The man jumped and said, "A Mercury Marquis, dark brown."

Doyle told Marco. "He has to be on 8th Street or in the parking lot by 8th. It would be in range for the bug."

"I'll get officers there, ASAP." He hung up and Doyle stood.

"The cavalry is coming, let's go watch," Doyle said.

"What about him?"

Doyle pulled his knife and cut the zip-cuff holding the man. "I think you'd better scoot, Skeeter may want to get his hands on you."

The man looked terrified and ran out the door going away from the area where Skeeter was hiding.

"Why'd you let him go?" Oscar asked.

"Skeeter was sacrificing the guy for his own plans, not very nice of him. I just gave him a chance to get away from Skeeter. Let's go see if Skeeter gets out of this."

They got to the door and Doyle stopped Oscar. "What's the matter?" Oscar asked.

"I'm just checking to see if Skeeter isn't double-crossing us. He could actually be across the street."

They scanned the area and saw no one, so they went out and down the sidewalk to the front of the Ottava Via restaurant on the corner of 8th and

Michigan. Doyle peeked around the building to see if he could spot a Marquis. He saw the car and there was someone in the front driver's seat. They were watching just as two police patrol cars roared up, closing off the side road from Michigan Avenue. Doyle could see down the side street where two more cars blocked the other way out. The police all converged using parked cars as shields, moving to the Marquis. Doyle saw Marco with the men and ran low to join him followed by Oscar.

There was no movement in the car. Either Skeeter was busy looking down or he didn't care. Everyone converged on the car, all yelling for him to get out, and show his hands. The person in the car held his hands out showing no weapon and then opened the door. The man stood and Doyle said out loud, "Damn, it's not him." He ran to the man and grabbed him by the shirt, pushing him onto the car hood and yelled, "Where's Skeeter?"

The man said nothing. Doyle punched him in the right side and the man cried out. Marco was standing by and said to the officers, "You see nothing." They all mulled around not paying attention to the men.

Doyle punched him again and he yelled, "He's gone. He left five minutes ago."

"How? On foot, or did someone picked him up?"

"He got picked up by Loco Lockie, in his car. He followed us to help, but Skeeter couldn't hear what you were saying so he left."

"And he left you to take the fall?"

"He told me to stay to draw attention from him. If I didn't, he said he'd kill me."

"Nice guy." Doyle pulled the man up and pushed him to the officers now watching. They cuffed him and put him in a car. Doyle went to look in the Marquis and saw a transceiver on the seat. It must have been how Skeeter could hear them. When Doyle dropped the bug in the water, it cut out, so Doyle figured that Skeeter thought his time was running out and he ran.

"Where's this other guy you said you had?" Marco asked.

"Oh, he escaped. He's long gone," Doyle smiled.

"You know, one day you're going to let the wrong person escape," Marco said with a grin.

"It's a curse. Now, see if you can get this character to talk about where Skeeter is hiding out."

Marco just shook his head and called for a tow on the Marquis. Doyle and Oscar went back to the office, when Doyle's phone buzzed signifying a message. He looked and it said "Front Door" so he clicked on the link and saw the front door of the office and it showed a picture of Doyle and Oscar going in. "It works. And there are three more notices with everyone who came and went since we put up the cameras. I like it."

"We're becoming techno detectives now," Oscar said.

"Is that like Robocop? Do we get steel suits?" Doyle said as his office phone rang. He went to answer and heard Skeeter's voice saying, "Well, you can be a good little detective once in a while. You may have messed up my plans, but I'm going to do my final blow to you. Just wait, and I'll call to invite you to the big blow-out," Skeeter said and hung up.

Doyle's Android phone had an app that recorded phone calls so he played the call back to Oscar. When it finished, Doyle said, "Sounds like he's not going to drop bodies on our door step anymore. Sounds like he's plotting something bigger. I hope he doesn't kill a group of people just for me."

"What about his threat to kill a cop?"

Doyle thought on that. "I think he may have tried that on us with this little plot around the corner. To draw us out and shoot you to piss me off. Maybe since it didn't work, he's moving his plan up. I'm not liking this."

"What do we do now?" Oscar asked.

"I hate to say it, but we wait. Maybe Marco can get something from the phone and from the guy we just nabbed. Since there's nothing to do here, shall we join Marco in his interrogating?"

"Sounds good." They both left the office and drove to Marco's precinct. They went in and were greeted by officers who recognize them. Doyle thought about how it would be nice to go back to his old precinct to say hi, if only Captain Cadeem was gone. They found Marco standing in the squad room talking to a uniformed officer. They waited until he was finished.

"Did you miss me already?" Marco said when he saw Doyle and Oscar.

"Missed you like the flu. Have you talked to our suspect yet?"

"I was just heading that way. I suppose you'd like to watch?"

"I was hoping to."

"If you promise not to beat up the perp, you can join me questioning him."

"I like that even better." They went to the hallway where the interrogation and observation rooms were. Marco pointed out an observation room for Oscar and he took Doyle into where the perp sat quietly. Marco sat across from him and Doyle stood behind him, leaning against the wall.

"According to your ID, you are Ramone Valisquis. One of the Cass Street boys, according to your record. What are you doing hanging with Skeeter Blain? He's not part of the Cass Gang."

He sat saying nothing. Doyle moved towards him and whispered in his ear. "That love tap I gave you at the car is nothing to what I'll do now. Why don't you answer the man's questions?"

"You can't hurt me, cop," he said quietly.

"I'm not a cop now. So I don't play by the rules," Doyle said and grabbed his wrist and gave it a twist under the table. Ramone winced in pain and said to stop. "I'll stop when you talk, now talk about Skeeter." Doyle stood and went to the wall behind Ramone.

Marco asked, "Why were you helping Skeeter?"

Ramone rubbed his wrist and said, "He's crazy, I don't want to end up like one of his victims. Since he's been back in town, he's killed three people, not including the one's he's throwing at the cop."

"He's not a cop, he's a P.I. and he doesn't like Skeeter. Where is Skeeter staying in town?"

"I don't know. He just appeared one day across the street from the clubhouse and called to me, Eddie, Loco, and Cruse. We heard him out, and with his threats, we decided to help him. As for where he's hiding out, I don't know. I did hear him say that he was going home soon, I guess he meant up north."

Doyle glanced at the mirror, figuring Oscar was back there watching. Doyle wondered if the big blow-out Skeeter promised was going to be up there. He'd have to call Mike to see what the situation was.

*

Chapter 23

"You don't know what Skeeter is up to or where he lives. I guess you aren't much good to us. All we have on you is illegal wiretap of an office. But that's a federal rap, so I guess I'll call the feds and turn you over to them."

Ramone's eye grew and he said, "Hey, let's not get crazy here. I cooperated with you, no need to bring the FBI in, is there?"

Doyle said, "I think we should give him back to Skeeter. He'll know what to do with him."

Now Ramone was looking panicked, "On second thought, call the feds, I'll be glad to talk to them."

"So we figured. You just rest in here until we decide what to do with you." Marco stood and Doyle followed him out of the room. Oscar joined them in the hallway.

"He's a low level punk, I'll make him sweat for a bit then cut him loose. Skeeter can figure out what to do with him," Marco said.

"Or he could just escape," Doyle said with a grin.

"That's your excuse. Now, let's find out what electronics got off the phone." Marco led them to the lab where they found a man sitting at a crowded counter covered in various electronic gear and apparatus.

"Larry, did you get anything from the phone I gave you?"

The man handed Marco a sheet of paper. He looked at it, and handed it to Doyle. "It's a list of numbers called by whoever used the phone. Not many, they probably just bought the thing this last week, when Skeeter got into town."

"Since Cruse had it, Skeeter may have provided phones to the men working with him," Doyle said.

"Makes sense, he needed to coordinate with them to keep ahead of you." Marco turned to Larry and asked, "Did you get a fix on the other phones?"

"I checked the other phone numbers listed on this phone, none had any GPS tracking working, so no go," Larry replied. "Your perp is still hiding out."

Doyle's phone played and he pulled it out. He excused himself and went out in the hallway. He had seen it was Mike and wanted privacy. "Hey Mike, what's up?"

"I called for two reasons, first, Amber said to tell you she misses you, lucky dog," he laughed. "The other is I wanted to know what's going on with Skeeter. We got the dental comparison and one of the bodies was Gloria. I had a warrant for his arrest made out for murder on all the bodies we found and the bodies around your cabin. Unless you have him in custody?"

"You give me too much credit. We don't have much to go on, but we have one more murder and one attempted so far down here. He's on the most wanted list in Detroit. He did say he was going to pull his big finale soon. So he may end up back there. Be on the watch for him."

"I will. Let me know if you find out anything." They finished and Doyle hung up. He turned back to the lab when he saw Oscar coming out.

"Marco got a call from one of his men at the hospital and they said Sammy is out of the deep end. The bullet didn't do any damage to any vital organs. He's resting and they hope by tomorrow they'll know more," Oscar said.

"That's good, one less victory for Skeeter. Mike called me and said they identified one of the women in the shallow graves as my old girlfriend, Gloria. It's sad, she was a bitch but she didn't deserve a shallow grave. I want Skeeter's balls."

Marco came out and said, "Larry got a fix on one of the phones. Out of four, one came to life for GPS.

Larry said it must have been turned on and the location is back at the Cass Street hangout."

"Shall we pay a visit?" Doyle asked.

"I've called for cars to converge, we better move fast before there's a gang war." Marco led them out of the building to their cars. Doyle drove behind Marco who had his flashers and sirens going.

"Aren't you going to turn yours on?" Oscar asked.

Doyle said, "Oh hell, why not." He reached over and flipped the switches, bringing the car's emergency signals to life.

They made it to the garage shortly after. Doyle could see the patrol cars parked across from the building. He figured Marco must have called to say to wait for him. Doyle parked behind Marco and they met on the sidewalk.

"You know I can cite you for using those lights, but I'll let it pass," Marco laughed. "Let's go get whoever has the phone. I called Larry and he said the GPS still has it located here."

They got to the door and Doyle said, "Listen, I sort of established a nice rapport with these guys, let me go first and tell your men to wait out here."

"It's your neck, go ahead." Marco waved to the door and stood aside.

Doyle opened the door as Marco told the officers to hold back. Doyle and Oscar walked into the darkness and over to the light. They could see about six men standing by the pool table talking. Doyle called to them as he got closer.

"Doyle, you're back? Did you get Skeeter?" The big man with the tats asked.

Doyle scanned the men, but didn't see Skeeter. "Hold on, I want to try something. Oh, this is my friend Marco, he's a cop, but he's cool." He turned to Marco and took the sheet of paper with the numbers out of his jacket pocket. "Which one was the one with the active GPS?" he asked Marco.

Marco pointed to the number and Doyle took out his phone and dialed it. They waited as the small black man asked what was going on. Suddenly the man next to him jumped when his phone rang.

Doyle went to the man and asked, "What's your name?" The man said nothing.

"He's Loco. He just got here a while ago. What the problem?" The big man asked.

"So, this is Loco? It seems Loco helped Skeeter to get away from the police earlier today," Doyle said, then asked the man, "Where did you take Skeeter after you drove him away? We know you did, we have Ramone in custody and he said you helped Skeeter escape."

The big man grabbed Loco and shook him. "Tell Doyle where you took Skeeter, you scum."

Loco still didn't say anything, then he said, "I'm more afraid of Skeeter then you, Monk."

"I'll make you afraid," he said and started punching the man. Then the other men took turns beating on him.

"Aren't you going to stop them?" Marco asked Doyle.

"He's their man, they'll get him to talk," Doyle replied.

Finally Loco started to beg, "Stop! I'll talk!"

Doyle went to the big man and put his hand on the man's shoulder. "Give him a breather. Let's hear what he has to say."

The man dropped Loco and stood back. Doyle knelt down to Loco sitting on the ground, face bleeding. "Talk to me. You have no more friends here. I can get you out without getting your ass killed," Doyle said quietly.

Loco looked to Doyle, "I don't know the address, but I can take you to him," Loco said, spitting out blood.

Doyle stood and said to the big man, "I like the way you make a man talk. I need him now to take us to find Skeeter. I'll return him after we're done with him."

"Take his sorry ass out of here, Doyle. Get Skeeter and put him down."

"I will." The two men fist bumped and Doyle told Marco to help him take Loco out. They pulled him up and took him to the exit.

Marco told two of the patrol cars to follow behind him. They took Loco to Marco's car and Doyle told Oscar to follow in his car. "Don't use the lights," he warned Oscar. They put Loco in back and Doyle got in the front, looking back to Loco. "Okay, show us the way or I'll take you back to big Monk."

Loco was still bleeding, so Doyle handed him a tissue from the front seat. Loco said," Go down Cass to Mack and over to John R. I'll tell you where after that."

They drove over to where Loco led them and up to an eight story building on John R. Doyle knew it was the former apartment building call The Jacobs, now just known as John R. Apartments. The cars all pulled up to the front, causing a few unsavory looking people standing in front to scatter. Marco gave orders to the men. He had one of the four stay at the front and told one other to go around back. The other two were to follow them in.

"Do you know where in the building Skeeter went?" Marco asked Loco as he handcuffed him inside the car.

"No, I just dropped him at the door, and he went in," Loco replied.

"Do you think he's still inside?" Doyle asked him from the door.

"Skeeter told me to come back to pick him up when he called me. He hasn't called yet."

Marco still had Loco's phone. He took it out and told Loco to call Skeeter and tell him he was there waiting. Loco gave him a look of terror and said, "He'll kill me, man."

"I think Monk wants to kill you, too. Your choice."

Loco was mulling it over and finally said, "I'll call."

*

Chapter 24

Marco handed Loco the phone and he pushed a couple buttons. He put the phone to his ear and waited. Marco grabbed the phone and switched it to speaker then held out in front of Loco. They could hear the phone ringing and then a voice came over the speaker, "Loco, I told you to wait for me to call."

"I got a problem and I think you need to come out now," Loco said.

"What the hell are you talking about?" Skeeter said.

Doyle moved across the street and scanned the building. On the fourth floor he suddenly saw someone go to the window and look out. It was Skeeter. Doyle stared at the man and saw Skeeter's eyes glaring back at Doyle. Then Skeeter moved away.

"He's on the fourth floor, front," Doyle yelled and ran back to Marco. Doyle and Oscar ran to the building as Marco told his men to follow.

Doyle was about one body length ahead of the rest, he wanted Skeeter badly. Marco told one more uniformed officer to go out the back and help the other cop back there and he followed Doyle. Doyle took the stairs two at a time, he didn't want to wait for the elevator. He did yell to Oscar to watch the elevator in case Skeeter goes that way.

Doyle's Justice

Doyle pulled open the fourth floor safety door and came out in the hall. He did a quick adjustment on which direction was the front and ran down to the second door on that side. He had seen Skeeter in the second window from the end. Marco and the last of the officers came up behind him.

Doyle smiled and said, "I'm not a cop, so I'll break and enter, if need be." He turned to the door and banged on it. They all stepped to the side in case someone inside was going to fire a weapon. The door opened and there stood a woman in a robe.

"Whatcha all want cops, I ain't done nuthin' wrong," she yelled.

Doyle pushed past her with his gun out front. Marco and the other cop spread out in the apartment checking and yelling 'clear' as they found no one else. Doyle went to the window and got a fix on where he was, it had to be the window where he saw Skeeter. Doyle went to the woman and grabbed her robe, pulling her to a wall and up against it.

"I'm not a cop, so I can beat the crap out of you, or you can tell me where Skeeter went?" he snarled in her face

"Who be Skeeter? I don't know no Skeeter," she wailed.

"The man who was just in this room, where is he?"

"You mean Billy, he split out two minutes ago, and he didn't pay me, son-of-a-bitch."

Doyle let her go and went back out the door. "He didn't go down the stairs, or we would have seen him." Doyle pulled his cell phone and speed dialed

Oscar. "Did Skeeter use the elevator?" he asked when Oscar answered. He got a negative. "Try all these doors to see if one is unlocked." Doyle pointed to the doors on the back side of the building. The cop found one door open and they all ran to it.

The room was vacant, but the window to the outside was open. Doyle ran to it and saw one cop on the ground and the other missing. "He took the fire escape and you've got a cop down and the other is gone." Doyle went out on the fire escape and downward, followed by Marco and the cop.

Marco told the officer to go tend to the cop on the ground. Doyle was looking around when they heard gunfire. He and Marco ran in the direction down an alley. They went all the way through and came to the end, emptying out on a street, where they found the other officer on the ground. He was still alive, Marco said, after checking him and pulling out his phone.

Doyle was scanning the area, but didn't see Skeeter. "Damn, this is getting ridiculous."

The last officer from the front came running around the building. Marco told him to watch the officer on the ground until the EMS got there. Marco went to Doyle as they looked around.

"He could have gone in any direction, Art. No sense in trying to follow," Marco said.

"Yeah, I know. I just want his ass so badly. Let's go back to the car and see if Loco can tell us anything more."

The two men left the officers to wait for the EMS, went around the front of the building to the car and found Loco with a knife in his chest. "What the hell?" Marco yelled.

"Skeeter must have waited for the officer to go around the side when he came running to us. Then Skeeter shived Loco," Doyle said.

"I feel sorry for this bastard, almost." Marco called for the coroner and turned to Doyle. "This creep is leaving a wake of death." Doyle agreed as Oscar was coming out of the building.

"Did you forget about me?" he said as he looked to Loco. "What happened to him?"

"I'll explain the whole sordid mess on the way," Doyle said to Marco, "I'll talk to you later, I'm heading to my office to re-group."

Doyle and Oscar went to the Charger and Doyle drove out. On the way, Doyle related to Oscar everything that happened in the apartment building and behind it.

"I miss all the good stuff," Oscar said.

"Wasn't much good stuff, two officers wounded, Loco is dead, and Skeeter is gone again."

"Why are we going back to the office?"

"I'm hoping Skeeter calls to gloat over the fact he got away. Maybe I'll find out his plans."

"Works for me," Oscar said. "I saw a nice phone recorder in my hunt for more electronic gadgets. We would have recordings of criminals calling us that way."

Doyle smiled and drove on. They arrived at the office and up to the door. Doyle unlocked it just as his phone buzzed, he pulled it out and saw the image of them at the door. "This thing works good. At least we know Skeeter hasn't been back here or in front." They went in, knowing it was safe.

"Doyle went to the front window and carefully looked out. He scanned the area and didn't see anything suspicious. Nobody sitting in cars, or Skeeter watching them.

"You do know Skeeter was on foot when he ran from the apartments and he has no friends in the Cass Street Gang to help him now," Oscar said.

"Yeah, I thought about that."

"Poor guy is all alone on foot in the big city. Maybe he'll get mugged," Oscar laughed.

"I'm sure the mugger will end up dead. Now all we can do is wait." Doyle sat and pulled his cell phone. He dialed Mike and waited until he answered. "Hey, Mike. Anything happening up there?"

"Not unless Skeeter is up here. I haven't heard anything yet," Mike replied.

"No, Skeeter is still down here. We just chased him while he was taking some time to enjoy a hooker. I hope he didn't get to finish."

"Well, that should frustrate him. Now he'll really want to take it out on you."

"Yeah, but he's always one step ahead of me. I'm the one getting frustrated. I just called to see if life was good up there and there were no more bodies at my cabin."

"Nope, my patrols have been watching the place and all is quiet. Amber has gone back to work; she said she was going stir crazy sitting around her apartment. Other than that, it's back to normal here. You should come up for a rest."

"I may need it with the way things have been going here. I'll fill you in when I come back up. Talk later, I'm waiting for Skeeter to call me to gloat about getting away so much."

"Just don't get killed," Mike said as the two men finished and hung up. Oscar was exploring the internet for more gadgets as Doyle sat back and looked around the office. He was happy now that he was on his own and not bowing to Captain Cadeem. He wondered what Cadeem was doing now that he didn't have Doyle to kick around. He probably found another whipping boy.

Doyle's desk phone rang and he picked it up. He said "Doyle Investigations," and listened. There was nothing said yet, but he heard breathing. "Skeeter, if this is you, just talk. I don't have time to listen to you breathing." Then he heard a laugh.

"Sorry Doyle, I'm just a little out of breath from walking all over Detroit. I didn't realize the city was so big on foot. And you disturbed my little tryst with the hooker, but you saved her life. I was going to take it when I finished. Now I'm good for a few days and you can relax. No more bodies until I get back on my feet and organize my big attack on your sensibilities. It will be great, something for the history books to put down."

"Criminal history books, you mean."

"Whatever, you will remember me for a long time. I'm going to make a big impression on you, Doyle. One that will live in your mind forever, so you won't forget what you put me through."

"Exactly what did I do to you that you hate me so much, Skeeter. Please explain."

"I will, but in due time, when I have your attention to my final plan," he said and hung up.

*

Chapter 25

Doyle felt the frustrations creeping back in and he hated it. Skeeter was playing mind games with him. What was he going to do for his big finale? Was it going to involve people he cared about? Was it going to happen here in Detroit or up by his cabin? Too damn many questions and no answers.

He turned to see Oscar at his desk working on his personal laptop, probably looking for more gadgets to modernize the office. Doyle figured when they get a few more clients, he'd purchase some decent computers for the office. They had an older model from the thrift shop that Marge used to keep track of all the stats on cases that they did have. Doyle felt like he was going to have to step up and bring in more work. This interruption by Skeeter wasn't helping business.

Doyle stood and went to the window looking out to Michigan Avenue. Traffic was light on the normally busy road, and the sun was shining. He felt like going out for a breath of air, but the air around there wasn't the best. It was the reason he took time to go to his cabin, just for the rest and fresh air.

Oscar came up behind him, breaking Doyle's concentration. "Whatcha thinking about, Art?"

"I'd like to get away. Far away and start over. Skeeter is really starting to get to me. What did I do to him that he's doing all this? The murders, and messing with my mind, plus we have no leads. Every associate of his has been caught or murdered. They haven't been much help to us. We don't know where he's hiding and what he's planning. It's so damn annoying."

"The police are working on it, too. Maybe they'll come up with something?" Oscar offered.

"I know that. Marco is hot on it also. I just feel like I should have more to go on. Skeeter just called and said he was regrouping for his big deal. He said we could rest until he was ready. How long? Bastard knows I won't rest while he sits back and enjoys making me crazy."

"I know what you need. You need to go visit Amber and get a little," Oscar said with a grin.

Doyle started laughing to himself. "I think that would be a good idea, but I don't know how well I could perform with Skeeter stuck in my head." Doyle turned away from the window and looked to Oscar.

"Maybe I will go up there. If Skeeter finds I've gone, he may follow. I would rather track him in the woods than here in the concrete jungle. Too many places to hide here. I'll put a sign on the door for Skeeter to let him know I've left the city. Feel like following me?"

"I'd welcome it. Shall I go pack?"

"It wouldn't hurt to have a few extra things. Go ahead, then meet me at my apartment. I just hope Skeeter hasn't found my apartment and dropped a body there. Be careful you're not followed."

"I'll see you in an hour and we can go," Oscar said and left.

Doyle sat back in his desk chair and pulled out his cell phone. He speed dialed Marco and explained that he was heading back north.

"If you do that, then Skeeter will most likely follow you. You better have your sheriff friend on alert," Marco said.

"I'm calling him next to warn him. I really need to get out of the city until this issue is solved. I don't have any idea why he wants to annoy me and I want to end this. So, hopefully, drawing him to my original stomping grounds may help."

"True, but remember, he's from up there too. He may have the same advantage you have. Down here you know the city from being a cop, and he's not real familiar with it."

"I know, but I feel I can move better up there. Less places to hide and less people to worry about."

"It only takes one person to be murdered. But I understand what you're doing. We haven't had any luck here with this mess, so maybe drawing him out up there may help."

"Thanks, Marco. I'll keep you informed if things go as I hope. I'll talk later," Doyle said and they finished. Doyle speed dialed Mike and waited.

"Hey, Art. You catch him yet?" Mike said when he answered.

"Nope, but I'm coming up to visit, and I'm hoping to draw him up there. It's too hard to find him down here, the city's too big and he's clever. So I just wanted to give you a heads up to be ready for whatever happens."

"I appreciate that. I'll alert my men and have them all familiarized with his photo. Most of my men aren't from around here, so they wouldn't know Skeeter," Mike said.

"Skeeter said he had some big thing he was going to do now. I don't know if he planned that for down here, but I hope I mess up his plans. He's sure messing with my head. I've done way more investigating in the last couple days and I'm not even getting paid for it."

Mike laughed and said, "Maybe you can sue him for his property, if you don't mind the shallow graves."

"No thanks, I like my cabin and I'll bite the bullet on this. Oscar is meeting me at my apartment and I'll have him follow me up to the cabin. I'll see you in a couple hours, after we get settled in." They hung up and Doyle made out a sign saying "*To whom it may concern, we've gone up to Oxford for a few days. Will return soon. Thanks!*" He took the tape and put it on the door. Hopefully Skeeter will see the paper and get curious.

Doyle went out back and over to his car, looking around for anyone watching. He drove to his apartment and found Oscar in the parking lot. Oscar didn't waste time. "Do you speed around in that heap you drive?" Doyle asked as they went to the back door of the apartment building.

"As I said, I know all the shortcuts," Oscar said with a big grin.

They went into Doyle's apartment and Oscar sat while Doyle threw a bag of clothes together. He checked his answering machine, but there were no messages. He looked to Oscar and said, "Let's get out of here."

They went to their cars and drove out. Doyle looked back to be sure Oscar was following. Doyle drove to the freeway and up to his cabin.

They arrived about an hour later and Doyle opened up the cabin to get some fresh air into it. He hadn't been gone that long, but he wanted it to air out.

Oscar plopped his bag down by the door and asked, "Are we flipping a coin for the bed?"

"I'll flip you if you think I'm giving up the bed. If the pull out couch was good enough for you to have sex in, then it's good enough to sleep in." Doyle looked at Oscar then realized that Oscar and Marie were the last to use the pull out bed. "On second thought, you can have the bedroom. You are a guest after all."

"Thanks, Art," he said quietly, probably thinking of Marie sitting dead on the porch.

Doyle put his bag in the bedroom and then said, "How about a nice meal? I know a good restaurant in Oxford."

"Sounds good. Are you going to call Mike to let him know we're here?"

"Yeah, I probably should, just so the patrol cars don't think we're Skeeter. Then we'll go eat, and after that we'll visit the Glory Hole Bar to see how Amber is doing."

"Sounds like a winner," Oscar said.

Doyle pulled out his cell phone and called Mike. "Hey Mike, Art here. Just giving you a heads up that Oscar and I are at the cabin and I've heard nothing from Skeeter. So warn your deputies that we are here and don't come in shooting."

Mike said to him, "It's all quiet here. I'll let you know if I hear anything. Are you going to visit Amber? She's working right now."

"Thanks for letting me know. I had planned on it. After Oscar and I go eat. Care to join us, if you aren't busy?"

"I may do that, it's almost my dinner time. Where are you going?"

"Oxford Diner."

"Okay, maybe I'll see you there," Mike replied. They finished up and Doyle took Oscar out to his car and drove to the restaurant.

The same bouncy waitress was there and she asked them what they would like. "How's the meat loaf today?" Doyle asked with a grin.

"Same as the last time, not great. I suppose you want fish and chips again?"

"Sounds good," Doyle replied. Oscar said one of the same for him. She bounced off after asking their drink order.

Mike came in and sat at the table. "What's the special today?"

"You should try the meatloaf," Doyle said, trying not to smile.

"Sounds good," he said as the bouncy waitress came over. "Hi Louise, I'll have the meatloaf."

She started to talk but Doyle just waved to her as Mike wasn't facing him, she stopped and smiled. "I'll get that order in for you, Mike," she said grinning.

"Cute girl," Oscar said.

"I've known her for years. Her dad is the coroner."

Doyle grinned and said quietly, "Glad I didn't order the meatloaf."

Mike gave him a puzzled look and sat back.

*

Chapter 26

Doyle covered the events of the last few days since he left Oxford. Mike sat listening to the story of murder and gangs with rapt attention. Oscar was enjoying the fish and chips while he listened.

"Now Skeeter calls me today and says he's getting a big show together for me. I can take a break, he says, but I'm sure he knows I can't take a break not knowing when he's going to strike. So I changed the dynamic by leaving the city. He'll have to regroup and move out here."

"Or, he already planned on moving out here," Oscar said, munching on his fish.

Doyle looked at this friend and said, "Very true. So we're getting ready to wait for the throw down. Whatever that will be. I just hope it's a quick throw down and one we can handle." Doyle looked at Mike and asked, "Do you still have men watching Skeeter's house?"

"Of course. But he's not going there if we're hanging around. I was thinking of pulling them back."

"It might be a good idea. Then if he contacts me, we can roll in to see if he's there."

"You aren't very good at this, are you?" Mike said with a grin. "Oh, and the meatloaf was very good. Louise told me what you were up to when I went to the restroom. She made sure it was fresh."

"Boy, she just lost her tip. Well, I want to go visit Amber and see if she's fresh."

"I'm for that," Oscar said.

Mike stood and said, "I have to get back to work. Thanks for paying for my meal." He put a five on the table. "That's her tip, don't touch it." He smiled and left.

"He loves doing that, stiffing me for his food. He hasn't changed. Shall we go see if we can relax?"

"I can relax, it's you I'm worried about," Oscar said, smiling. "Maybe Amber will relax you."

"I certainly hope so," Doyle said and stood. He put a ten on the table, just to show up Mike. They went to pay the bill and left.

On the way to the bar, Oscar asked, "Don't you worry that Skeeter may go after Amber again?"

"I plan on watching her carefully this time."

"Just don't get distracted."

"I'll be careful. Besides, I have you for back up."

They arrived at the Glory Hole and parked. "Do you want to make a grand entrance or just sneak in?" Oscar asked.

"I'm just going to go in and sit at the bar. I'll let nature take its course." Doyle smiled and went to the door. He entered and went straight to the bar. The place was fairly empty since it was still early, so the bar was wide open.

"Art!" came a loud yell from the other end of the bar. Amber came running down and almost jumped over the counter. She latched on to his shirt as he was sitting and pulled him up over the bar and planted a long kiss on him.

Oscar sat next to him and said, "I'll have what he's having."

Amber broke away from Doyle and laughed. "I'm sorry, Oscar." She pulled him over and gave him a big kiss. "Is that better?"

"I'm happy," Oscar replied.

"So, are you back to stay?" she asked Doyle.

"No, I still have a business in Detroit, as you know, but I'm here to relax."

"Did you find your killer?"

"Well, that's another problem. Do you have a little time to take a break?"

Amber looked down the bar and yelled, "Harvey, can you watch the bar?"

165

Doyle's Justice

The man agreed and Amber came over the bar counter butt first. She dropped into Doyle's arms and gave him another kiss. He lifted her and set her down on the floor. "Let's go sit."

"Harvey, take care of my man Oscar, it's on me, and bring us a couple cold Millers," she said and followed Doyle to a booth. They sat and Doyle waited silently while Harvey brought them the beers.

"So what's up, gorgeous?" Amber asked.

Doyle wasn't sure if she was totally over being kidnapped by Skeeter, but he had to know. "I'm going to ask this, since I'm here to protect you now, but how are you feeling about the incident with Skeeter?"

She looked distressed and sat back in the booth. She stared at the table and was quiet. Doyle gave her the time to collect her thoughts. She was silent for a while and Doyle could see she was searching her soul or mind for the words.

"I was very scared and concerned that I was going to be dead shortly after he took me. I didn't know what he would do. Rape me, or just kill me. I listened to him in the duct work talking to someone as I told you before you went downstate. I knew then he was going to use me to get at you. I didn't know what he had done until you told me that he murdered Marie, poor woman." She looked at Oscar sitting by himself at the bar. "Poor Oscar. I would have been traumatized seeing her dead like he did."

"Oscar is pretty tough, but I think it bothered him. They shared a close relationship for the night.

Not like he had an attachment to her, but it still hurt him."

She looked at Doyle and locked eyes with him. "You have to stop him."

"I intend to. But the problem is, he may be coming back up here from Detroit."

She sat back and closed her eyes. "I don't think I can stand to have him around again. I might kill him myself."

"Do you have a gun?" Doyle asked.

"Of course, doesn't everyone up here have one?"

"Well, be careful you don't shoot me," he laughed.

"Do you know when he's coming back?"

"Actually, I'm not even sure if he is coming back here. He may stay in Detroit and challenge me to come back there. I think he's going to come here, but I've been known to be wrong."

"Let's take care of him, when he gets here," she said.

"You are one dangerous woman," Doyle said with a grin.

Doyle looked over to the door when it opened and in came a very huge man. He recognized him as Hector, the drummer from the band and a man he arrested years ago in Detroit. Hector looked over and saw Doyle.

"Damn, Doyle, you're back," the mountain said and came over. "Hey, Amber. Are you two a couple now?"

"We're still exploring our options, Hector," Amber said.

167

"Well, I think you two are a cute couple. Doyle, you going to hang around this time?" he asked.

"For a while, yes. I have to catch a killer and he may be coming to the area."

"Wow, you need help, let me know. I got friends that would be able to help too."

"I may do that, thanks," Doyle said.

"Well, got to go set up to play. Talk later," Hector said and went off.

"Good to have friends like him," Amber said.

"We should get back to Oscar. He looks lonely. Are you going to be alright with Skeeter coming back?" he asked.

"As long as you protect me, I will." She leaned over and kissed him.

They stood and went back to the bar. Amber went around to the back.

"So, is she going to be able to handle Skeeter?" Oscar asked.

"I think she'll be all right. But we need to watch her. Skeeter knows her importance to me. Maybe I shouldn't have come back here."

"Art, you needed to draw him out. This is the perfect place to do so. It will be all right, we'll get him."

Doyle loved Oscar's complete faith in everything no matter how bad it could be. Oscar was Doyle's conscience.

The room was starting to fill with customers and the band started playing. "Are you going to take Amber back to the cabin?" Oscar asked.

"I don't know. It might not be a good idea. But I don't want you to go there alone."

"We could go get a couple motel rooms to spend the night," Oscar said.

Doyle laughed and said, "That isn't such a bad idea. We'll work it out later."

Amber came to Doyle and asked in his ear, "Would Oscar be alright if I send another woman to spend some time with him?"

Doyle thought on it. "I don't think he'd object. I'll subtly ask him and let you know."

She went off and Doyle turned to Oscar, "What would you say if I could arrange for you to hook up tonight?"

"With a woman?"

"No, a good looking man. Of course, a woman."

"Art, I'm over Marie. It was unfortunate, but I will go on. If I have the opportunity to hook up with a woman, I'll take it."

Doyle smiled and looked to Amber, watching him. He nodded his head and smiled. She disappeared from behind the bar then came up next to Doyle and Oscar. She had a woman with her, and introduced her to Oscar.

"Oscar, this is Lily. She's a nurse and my friend. Could you keep her company, she's alone tonight."

Oscar turned on the stool and smiled. "It's a pleasure to meet you, Lily." He stood and asked her to sit on the stool. He moved over to the next stool and turned to her.

"Amber tells me you're a private investigator?" she asked.

"Yes, I have my own agency in Detroit," he said. Doyle laughed and winked at Amber.

*

Chapter 27

The band played a number of slow dances, probably at Amber's request. Amber was finished tending bar for the night, so she dragged Doyle to the dance floor to rub bellies. She had nice moves when the songs got faster and Doyle enjoyed watching her gyrate. She reminded him of a stripper he once knew down in Detroit. Now, she had moves a man could enjoy.

They moved to a table and sat talking about different subjects. Jobs, hobbies and such, mostly Oscar bragging to Lily. Doyle let him have his moment.

Doyle's cell phone rang and he pulled it out, excusing himself to go out to the vestibule at the front door, for the quiet. He saw it said Marco, so he answered. "Hey, have you caught Skeeter yet?"

"No, but we almost had him. I talked to Cruse again and he remembered Skeeter saying he liked pizza at Giovanni's. I had a stakeout set up and he came waltzing in tonight. Unfortunately, one of the cops on the stakeout was a rookie and got anxious to nab him. He spooked Skeeter and he ran. The men outside were taken by surprise and missed him

170

coming out. So he's still down here, but I can't say if he'll stay. So you have a little breather for the night. He seems to be still on foot, unless he can hotwire a car."

"His house up here is being watched, so he doesn't have a place to go. I don't think he has any friends up here to hide with, but I'll have to check around and see. He may hole up in a motel. I don't know if he has a credit card or cash. Might be a good idea to check to see if he has a credit card."

"Already did. If he has one, it's not in his name. No cards, no finances, no personal history other than a driver's license. This guy is a ghost. I just hope he haunts somewhere else. I'm assigning too much manpower to finding him. We're getting tapped out on overtime."

"Well, do what you can. I want his ass nailed down here or there. I'll let you know if I hear anything." They finished and Doyle went back to the table.

"What's up?" Oscar asked.

"Marco was just checking in, nothing important." Doyle didn't want to bring up the subject of Skeeter in front of the women.

It was getting late and Amber was wearing down. She said to Doyle quietly in his ear, "Lily has an apartment next to mine. That's how I know her. We could go to the building and you can come to my place and Oscar can go to Lily's. She already told me she was interested in him."

"Let's play it by ear and go to your place and see what they want to do." Doyle looked to Oscar who was now snuggling with Lily. "I hate to interrupt you two, but we're thinking of leaving and going to Amber's place."

"Sounds good," Lily said and glanced at Oscar. "Are you ready to go?"

They all agreed and left the building. Oscar went with Lily in her car and Amber led the way in her car. Doyle followed, thinking about being able to rest tonight, without having to worry about Skeeter.

Doyle ended up in Amber's apartment. Lily asked Oscar if he wanted to see her collection of Hummel figurines. Doyle was sure Oscar wasn't going to look at figurines, other than her. They all said their goodnights and went off.

Amber turned to Doyle in her living room and said, "Are you going to be able to relax tonight?"

"I am. Skeeter is still down in Detroit, so it'll be quiet for the night."

"Good," she said with a smile and walked to the bedroom, shaking her beautiful rear end. Doyle had to follow.

Doyle woke with a start from a bad dream. He hated dreams and wished he couldn't remember them. They put him in situations that he couldn't control and he never had a gun in those situations. He sat up and looked over at Amber sleeping peacefully, the light from the outer room illuminating her face. He swung his feet over the side and went to the kitchen to see what was in the fridge. He found four cold Millers so he took one. It was just after three in the morning, so a beer wouldn't kill him.

He sat on the couch and took a swig of the beer. He wondered what Skeeter was up to. Was he sleeping or was he plotting how to make Doyle's life miserable? Doyle had a flash of the face from the woman hung up in front of his office. Bastard, he thought of Skeeter. That woman had nothing to do with Doyle, and shouldn't have been murdered just for Skeeter's pleasure. He wasn't going to go easy on Skeeter if he got his hands on him.

He turned to the hallway when he heard a movement and realized he didn't have his gun. It was Amber. He smiled and waited until she raided the fridge for a beer. She came to him and sat close.

"Can't sleep?" she asked.

"Bad dream. I'm under pressure with this case, and it's hard to keep my head straight. If I could just turn off my brain when I sleep, it would be so nice."

"You need to try Zen meditating before you sleep. It moves your head to a different plane and it helps you to sleep. I do it a lot, when I'm not drunk and forget to meditate."

"I'll try it sometime. Do you have a secret word you say to get the karma flowing?"

"That's not karma, I have a relaxing word that I use, better than 'ooom' and a lot simpler. I just say Oh..oh..God…so good…don't stop…" She smiled as Doyle hit her arm.

"You already said that. Did you sleep well?"

"Yes, and I had a nice dream about you."

"And that wasn't a bad dream?"

"Nope, you were very good in my dream as you are in real life. I'm going back to bed and meditate. You can join me if you like."

She got up and left him on the couch. He sat there until he heard her calling out, "Don't stop…Ohhh." He downed the beer and got up.

Early the next morning, Doyle felt Amber slide out of bed. He did sleep well after the early morning meditation. He opened his eyes and saw Amber, naked, moving to the door and out. He sat up and looked for his clothes.

He put on his pants and left the bedroom, going to the kitchen where he found Amber now wearing his shirt. What was with women who liked to wear men's shirts while naked? Doyle blamed Shania Twain for her song, "*I Feel Like a Woman*" that mentioned wearing men's shirts. She did also mention short skirts, so it wasn't all bad.

Amber was making eggs and Doyle slipped up behind her, causing her jump. "I could have thrown these eggs at you," she said smiling. "You'd have egg on your face."

"Wouldn't be the first time. I slept well after we meditated. No bad dreams this time. I need to do some investigating today. Do you have to work?"

"I'm off until tonight. What did you have in mind?"

"Well, I want to protect you, so what better way than to keep you around me. I'll see what Oscar has to say and we'll go from there." Doyle removed his shirt from Amber and she had on her undergarments.

174

"Darn, I was hoping you'd still be naked. But work calls and I have a killer to track down."

They both dressed and Doyle went to the door when he heard knocking. He peeked through the peep hole and saw Oscar's ugly mug. He opened the door and said good morning. "How did you sleep?" he asked Oscar.

"In a bed, of course. I usually sleep in a bed. But sometimes I sleep on a couch, especially when I visit you."

"Wise ass. Did you and Lily get along?"

"Yes, very well. I may marry that woman," he said with a grin.

"Sure, make her wife number…what is it…four?"

"Who counts when you're in love?"

Doyle laughed and said, "No comment. Are you ready to go see what we can find on Skeeter?"

"Where do we start?" Oscar asked, sitting on a kitchen chair.

"I want to see if he had any friends around here. Maybe they would know more about him."

Amber came out from the hallway and said good morning to Oscar. "How did you get along with Lily?"

"Don't ask. He wants to marry her now," Doyle said.

"Don't worry about that. Lily has already told me she wants nothing to do with marriage."

"Hear that, Oscar. She's perfect for you," Doyle said.

Oscar held up his middle finger.

"So, where are we going to?" Amber asked.

"I think we need to visit Mike at the sheriff's office to see what he has. Then work our way from there."

"Do you think looking around here will help find Skeeter?" Oscar asked. "He is still in Detroit."

"I want to see if he has any friends up here who would let him hide out. His house is being watched, so he would need a place to go if he comes back. Which I think he will."

"Especially when he reads your note on the door of the office."

"Yep, he'll be coming back here."

Doyle's cell phone played its theme and he saw it was Mike. "Mike, what's up?"

"I just got a phone call from Skeeter."

*

Chapter 28

"Now why would he call you?" Doyle asked.

"Well, he said you weren't in your office and he didn't know your cell phone number, so he called me. I'm not going to be your answering service, so give him a number he can call you at."

"Like hell I am. I don't want him to know my private number. What did he say?"

"Well, he said he had his plan all mapped out and you would really enjoy it. I asked him where he was going to implement his plan, he laughed and said that was for you to find out."

"Damn, I may have to give him a number to reach me at. Did you get a return number from his call?"

"Yep, he said it was where you could reach him. He also said it had no GPS, so don't bother. We don't have the equipment to track him from the cell towers, so he's somewhere in Detroit, or so he said."

"Give me the number and I'll call him." Mike repeated the number as Doyle entered it in his notepad.

"Are you going to call him, so he doesn't call me again? He gives me the creeps. That voice of his is grating."

"I know, I've talked to him a few times. I'll call and let you know what he said. We'll probably come in to the station later, so expect us."

"Us? You and Oscar?"

"I may have Amber with us. I'm protecting her while I'm here."

"You are so noble. What a guy. See you later," he said and hung up.

Doyle hung up and looked at the number. He went to the dining table and sat.

"What's up?" Oscar asked.

Doyle told him about Mike's call.

"He's moving on," Oscar said.

"Yeah, but where to. So, I'll call and find out. It's my best bet. Now be quiet while I talk to the evil one."

"Go for it," Oscar said.

Amber was listening to the conversation and sat at the table. "I'll be quiet, too," she said. Doyle smiled at her and dialed the number after setting the caller ID block. He didn't want Skeeter to have his number right now. He put the phone on speaker, so Oscar could hear.

The phone rang a couple times then it was answered. Doyle waited, then Skeeter said, "You're blocking the call, Doyle. Don't you want me to call you?"

"Hell, no. I don't want to hear your annoying voice. You want to call me, call my office and leave a message. I'll get the notification and call you back."

"You're an arrogant prick, Doyle. I'm trying to have fun with you and you don't want to play nice."

"I don't play with killers, Skeeter."

"Stop calling me that!" Skeeter yelled into the phone.

"What, Skeeter? Okay, I'll call you Bill from now on. Is that good Bill?"

"That's my damn name, use it. You and that bitch Gloria started that name and it stuck. Do you realize how much that bothered me? Skeeter! It's not a name, it's a bug, for Christ's sake."

"Is that why you want to see me squirm?"

"It's the one big thing, yes."

"Bill, I never started calling you Skeeter. It was Gloria, and you took care of her, didn't you? Did being called Skeeter scar you for life? Are you reaching out to get revenge for a name? You're a sick person, Bill."

"Shut up, Doyle. I have my plan all set up for you. I just need two things to complete it. You'll find out soon enough," he yelled and hung up.

Doyle hung up and looked to his companions. "Well, I think that answers one mystery. He doesn't like being called Skeeter."

"I wouldn't either," Amber said.

Doyle looked at her and smiled. "No, it's not a good name for a human. But it's perfect for a sadistic killer. I guess we wait until he gets his plan finished. I'm not looking forward to this."

They got ready to go out, and Oscar said his goodbye to Lily, who was heading to work. Doyle started his car and everyone got in, then he drove to the sheriff's station and parked.

"Did you call Skeeter?" Mike asked as they came up to his desk.

"Yes, I can't call him Skeeter anymore. He wants to be called Bill, so if you hear me say that name, you'll know. I guess he associated me with Gloria's indiscretion. I'm sorry Gloria met with this fate, but she was mean."

"Doesn't excuse murder. I remember Gloria as being a bitch too, but she didn't deserve to die. Elwood wasn't able to get an exact cause of death, her body was badly decomposed. He doesn't have all the fancy scientific toys you big city cops have. What did Skeeter – sorry, Bill – have to say?"

"Same as he threatened the last couple days. He has this big production number he wants to present to me to make me regret ever calling him Skeeter. Even if I didn't start calling him that until this last week.

179

Oh, hell, I'm still going to call him Skeeter. He's an annoying little bug, buzzing in my ear. He still won't say where he's going to exact his revenge on me."

"I hope it's in the city. I don't need the aggravation up here," Mike said with a grin.

"You know, you're getting lazy. Do you remember any friends Skeeter had back then?"

Mike thought a moment, "I seem to remember one guy, name was George Klepper, who did hang with Skeeter. He's still around. I saw him at the gas station on the corner of Lapeer and Lincoln, across from Holy Cross Lutheran Church. He was working there, I think. He was cleaning the garbage cans."

"It's a start, thanks Mike." He turned to his friends and said, "Shall we go investigate?"

They left and drove to the gas station, it was a Sunoco. Doyle parked on the side and they went in. Doyle went to the man at the counter and asked for George.

"He's in the back," the man said. "George, someone here to see you." he yelled. He smiled at Amber and said, "What ya up to, Amber?"

"Just investigating, Earl. Haven't see you in the bar lately."

"Yeah, the wife has grounded me. I'll be back one day," he said, just as a man came out from the back.

Doyle recognized him even though he had aged poorly. "George, do you remember me? Art Doyle."

George's eyes widened and he stuttered, "Yeah…I do…what do you want?"

"Some information, can we go outside?"

Earl said from the counter, "Take a break, George."

George led them out and to the side of the building. "I know why you're here, Doyle. Bill called and warned me about you. You want to kill him, don't you?"

"George, I want to stop him from killing people. He's already murdered two people here and left them by my cabin. And then he went to Detroit and murdered a woman there. Sheriff Mike Twain has a warrant out for him after finding eight bodies buried on Bill's property. Yes, George, I'd like to see him dead, but it's not my job to kill him. When did he call you last?"

George hesitated and then said, "Yesterday. He asked me if he could stay with me for a couple days. I told him I was living with my mother and it was her house. I didn't think she would let him. He asked me if I could go rent him a motel room for a couple days. I said I would. It's all arranged."

"I'll have you talk to Sheriff Twain about that. Can you get off, or shall I have him come here?"

George opened his mouth to reply when there was a shot from a distance and George's chest exploded from a bullet. Doyle grabbed Amber and pushed her down behind a dumpster as he and Oscar were watching to see where the shot came from.

"Damn it! He's here," Doyle shouted. He looked around and saw a car pull out from the church parking across the street. Earl came running out and saw them off the side. "Earl, call 911 and get an EMS

here. Stay with George until they get here. I didn't
check, but he may still be alive."

He helped Amber up and then they ran to
Doyle's car. He drove out in the direction the car
went, but he didn't see the car. He couldn't identify
the car, it was the same as a dozen other cars. They
all looked alike. "Oscar, call Mike and tell him what
happened. And warn him Skeeter is in town, to get a
BOLO out."

Oscar called Mike and explained. He hung up
and said, "Now we have to find the motel that George
made the reservation at."

"I think now that Skeeter saw us with George, he
may regroup, thinking we know about the motel. I
wonder where he got the car?"

Doyle turned around and drove back to the gas
station. When he pulled in, he saw an EMS, an
Oxford Police car and a sheriff's car. Doyle parked
and they got out. Mike was talking to an officer of
the Oxford Police.

"Art, everywhere you go there's a shooting,"
Mike said. "Art, this is Sergeant Dave Wilkinson,
Oxford Police."

"I'm surprised they let you back in Oxford, Art,"
the officer said.

"Can't keep me away, Dave. How have you
been?"

"Good, long time no see. Mike was filling me in
on your adventures. Are you going to drag crime into
our quiet little city?"

"I'll try to lure it out to my cabin where the
sheriffs have to take charge," Doyle replied.

"Good. George lived, but he'll be out for a while. Let's talk about this so I'll be ready."

*

Chapter 29

The men talked while Amber and Oscar went into the gas station building. Oscar was feeling hungry so he got a hot dog from the counter slow cooker. He got one for Amber who was talking to Earl, explaining what they were doing.

"I remember Bill, he was a real ass. So, he's turned to killing people, I would figure him for that," Earl said.

Amber took the hot dog from Oscar and took a bite. Earl said it was on the house for both of them. They thanked him and went out. Doyle was still talking to the men and glanced over to Oscar and Amber as they came up.

He turned to them and said, "Well, we now know Skeeter is planning his finale here. I think we need to go to the cabin and wait it out. He'll probably come there for it. I've got some shotguns in the trunk we can use. Amber, I think I want you around me, he knows too much about you, and if you go home, he may pay you a visit."

"I'll trust your decisions," she said and kissed his cheek.

"Are we done here, Dave?" Doyle asked the officer.

"I can't think of any reason for you to stay around Oxford if you have a murderer following you. Your cabin is a good place to go, lead him away from us," he laughed.

"Protect and serve is the motto, except in your case. Good to see you again, Dave. We'll have to get together and socialize."

"Sounds good," he replied and said goodbye to Mike. He went to his car and drove out.

"You're going to stay in your cabin now?" Mike asked.

"I guess that's the only way we can end this. Skeeter wants me and this way he'll know where I am. Keep an eye out around the area, especially Baldwin Road."

"I will. Be careful." He left them and drove out.

Doyle looked at Oscar just finishing his hot dog. "I was thinking of treating everyone to a meal of fish and chips, but I see you ruined your appetite."

"Hey, I can force fish and chips. That hot dog wasn't very filling."

"Nothing fills you, Oscar," he said and looked to Amber. She agreed she could eat. Doyle took them all to the Oxford Diner and found Louise was working. The bouncy waitress came to take their orders.

"Don't tell me, fish and chips?" she said.

"Three of them," Doyle replied and she went off.

An hour later, with stomachs full, they drove out towards the cabin.

"Are you going to stop for beer?" Oscar said.

"I think we'll bypass beer until Skeeter tips his hand. I want a clear head."

Amber grinned and said, "I've seen you handle pretty tough fights while drinking."

"Yeah, I do get tough in those situations, but Skeeter is clever and I don't want my head messed by him and alcohol."

They arrived at the cabin and went in carefully. Doyle looked first and then had Oscar sweep the place for traps. They found everything as they left it and relaxed in the lawn chairs on the front porch. It was starting to get dark, a twilight of brilliant orange showcased across the water as the sun went down.

"Red sky at night, sailor's delight, red sky by morning, sailor's warning," Oscar quoted.

"I hope the red sky at night is a good sign," Doyle said as his cell phone rang. It was Mike. "Did you miss me already?"

"I would never miss you with my gun," he said with a laugh. "But, I called about another matter. There was a break-in at a construction company down below Oxford and a quantity of dynamite was stolen. I don't know if this has anything to do with Skeeter, but be real careful now. Keep an eye out around your cabin and call me if you hear anything. Be careful, Art."

Doyle was silent, thinking about what Mike said. "Thanks Mike, I'll be alert and call you if something breaks. You better come running fast."

"I will, talk later," Mike said and hung up. Doyle sat back in the lawn chair and stared out to the water, worrying about what Skeeter may be up to. This was not good. Dynamite. What could Skeeter be up to? Doyle stood as Oscar asked him who called.

"Mike, he was giving me a warning about Skeeter. He may, and I say *may*, have stolen some dynamite from a construction company. Mike has no proof, but it seems like something Skeeter might do. He just wanted to warn us. So we need to be on the watch for anything."

"What would he want to blow up?" Oscar asked.

Doyle looked at his cabin and hoped it wasn't that. "Skeeter said he had a big production to do. I guess fireworks and explosions would be a big production. We'll have to take watch tonight, so why don't you go get some sleep and I'll wake you around one, and you can take over for a couple hours."

"You really think I'll sleep after hearing that? I think I can stay up for one night to watch for him," Oscar argued.

"I guess we'll both be waiting up tonight." Doyle looked at Amber sitting quietly in her chair. "Why don't you go in and rest?"

"I'm not going to rest. You'll wake me up to move fast and I'll be stumbling around half asleep. No thank you. I'll wait with you two."

"Okay then, the three Musketeers will be ready for battle." He stood up and continued, "We need to form a plan to watch around the cabin. Skeeter can slip up behind the cabin like he did to drop the first body. So we'll need to patrol the area. I have flood lights in the back, so I'll turn them on for the night.

I'll be damned if Skeeter gets anywhere near us tonight, or any night."

Oscar stood and the two men walked around the back to check it out. Amber followed them from behind. Doyle had turned the flood lights on and the woods behind the cabin glowed with a spooky effect. There was a mist wafting through the area, making it difficult to see. All the shadows seemed to move fluidly, appearing as if someone was moving through the trees.

"We need to be alert. If he comes from Baldwin, from the back, we'll need to know. I wish I had motion sensors out here."

"It's not something you can take care of now, Art," Oscar said.

"I know, but I really want to catch him."

"And, you will. You are the hero of this story and you will take down the bad guy," Oscar said.

Doyle smiled and said, "Thanks, Oscar, you keep me focused."

They went back to the front and Doyle pulled the lawn chairs off the porch and set them up on the lawn facing the cabin. "Now we can watch the area around the cabin."

About two hours later, Doyle's phone rang. The caller ID said it was Mike. Doyle answered. "What's up, Mike?"

"I got a call from Skeeter again. He said to have you call him. We have to stop meeting like this. Let me know what he wanted."

"I will, Mike, thanks," Doyle said and hung up. He looked to Oscar and Amber. "Here we go." He dialed the return number and waited. Oscar stood and went over to Doyle to listen. Doyle put the phone on speaker. The phone on the other end rang and then it was answered.

"Doyle, I don't like your answering service. He's not very nice," Skeeter said.

"Screw you, Skeeter. Yes, I said Skeeter. You don't deserve to be called Bill. What do you want?"

There was a silence, then he spoke, "I need you in town, Doyle. I'm ready to blow up a favorite place of yours. Yes, you know I stole the dynamite, so don't play dumb. You want to save the cute waitress, then come into town, alone. I said alone, or I'll blow up the restaurant. And don't call your friend at the Sheriff's Department, that will make me blow up the place. I want you alone, to take care of business, finally. You and me, man to man. Can you hack it?"

Doyle didn't know what to do. Skeeter had the answers that Doyle needed to know, so he figured it must be the place. Blow up the restaurant with Louise and all the customers inside. It would be enough to make Doyle's blood boil. Skeeter had the upper hand now.

"Can you handle me, Skeeter?" Doyle challenged.

"Try me, asshole. I'll be glad to take you down. If you can best me, you'll save the restaurant. But, if you lose, I'll blow up all those nice people. Can you handle it?"

"I'll be there in ten minutes." Doyle hung up and turned to Oscar. "You have to stay and watch Amber and the cabin. Skeeter has challenged me and it's going to end there."

"Art, are you sure he's being honest?"

"What else could be his big production, other than taking out the restaurant? He wants to go out in a blaze and I'm not going to let him," Doyle said.

"I don't like leaving you alone in this," Oscar said.

"I appreciate that my friend, but this whole thing boils down to him and me. It has to be what he's been waiting for. I'll be all right. Watch Amber," Doyle said and went to his car.

Oscar dialed Mike and told him what was happening. "I don't like it, but if Skeeter sees you, he may blow up the restaurant. You decide, I'm staying here and watching the cabin and Amber. Call me if things go bad."

*

Chapter 30

Doyle arrived at the restaurant and didn't see Skeeter. He expected Skeeter would be bold enough to stand out front if he had the dynamite planted. He got out of the car and went up to the building. He looked in the front window and saw Louise and the customers all doing what they were expected to do. Doyle looked around and realized he had been duped.

Doyle's Justice

"Damn you, Skeeter!" he yelled and ran back to his car. He pulled out of the parking lot and flipped on his flashers and siren. He roared up the road back to his cabin. He pulled out his cell phone and speed dialed Oscar, but got no answer. "Damn you, Skeeter!" he yelled.

Doyle arrived and parked down the road from the cabin. He shut off the car and got out. He couldn't see any movement around the cabin, but it was now dark so it was hard to see. The flood lights were out, which was not what Oscar would have done. He slipped through the darkness to the cabin and listened for sounds. He heard none.

He moved to the side of the cabin and listened again, he could hear talking. He got closer to the front and listened. "Doyle is a fool, but he'll be smart enough to realize I'm not waiting for him. Now, let's see if he's smart enough to come back here. I'll take both him and you two out. He'll come rushing in and he'll blow all of you up. What fun. I just need to flip this switch and the bomb is armed. When he comes in, he'll trip this wire, activating the bomb. By the time he tries to free you from the ropes, the bomb will blow. I want him to panic and try to beat the timer." There was a moment's silence, then Skeeter spoke again, "There, the bomb is armed. All we need now is Doyle."

Doyle moved to the front door and waited, listening. Oscar said, "What makes you think Doyle will fall for your trap?"

"Because I'm clever and Doyle is dumb," Skeeter said.

Bob Moats

Doyle was up on the porch by the door and said, "I don't think you're very smart, Skeeter."

The room went silent, Doyle heard movement towards the door and he waited, holding his Sig out.

The door slowly opened but there was no one there. Doyle fired behind the door through the wall. He stopped, thinking about where Oscar and Amber were in the room. Doyle held his gun out and ran into the room, scoping around. Oscar yelled to watch out for the trip wire on the floor. Doyle looked down and saw the wire stretched from a box chained to the couch over to the dining table. He carefully stepped over it and quietly asked where Skeeter was.

Oscar said quietly, "Skeeter went into the bedroom."

Doyle approached Oscar and Amber who were tied to chairs. Amber was unconscious and Doyle whispered to Oscar to take her out to his car down the road and to stay with her. Doyle used his folding knife to cut the ropes holding Oscar and Amber and went to the bedroom door. Doyle nodded to Oscar to move out. Oscar picked up Amber and went out the door. Doyle waited, giving Oscar time to get to the car. He then said, "Skeeter, I know you're in there. The windows don't open so there's no escape. Do you want to surrender like a man, or shall I just trip the wire and leave you in there?"

He waited, then heard Skeeter say, "You came back a little quicker than I thought you would, I was going to hide outside waiting for you. You're not such a big man, Doyle. You wouldn't help me when

191

those three boys were beating on me. You just stood watching."

"I don't know what you're talking about?"

"Patrick Morrison and his gang of thugs. They got me in the parking lot at school and beat on me. I saw you just standing there watching. You did nothing."

Doyle suddenly remembered the incident. He also remembered the three boys were jocks and bigger than he was. He wasn't about to take them on. "Is that what this is about? You say I gave you the name Skeeter and didn't come to your rescue. Well, excuse me for not getting my ass kicked, too. You are a murderer, Skeeter. I'll always see the faces of Tammy, Marie, and the insurance man. Let's not forget the innocent woman jogging by my office, who you killed. And Gloria, she wasn't a nice person, but she didn't deserve a shallow grave. Not to mention the other women you buried on your property. A stone cold killer you are, Skeeter. Who will give your victims the justice they deserve?"

"You think you can, Doyle? What say we settle this like men and I'll give you the beating those guys gave me. Man to man, fists only. Prove you can best me, Doyle, or are you still a wimp?"

"How does this play out, Skeeter?" Doyle asked.

"You put your gun down and we meet face to face, fists only. Can you hack it?"

Doyle thought about it. Unless Skeeter had more hand-to-hand combat training than he did, he should be able to take Skeeter. "Okay, you're on. I'll put my gun on the couch. You come out slowly, no weapon, then we'll do this."

"Agreed. I can see you through the door crack, so put your gun down. I want to kick your ass, Doyle."

Doyle went to the couch and set his Sig down. He turned and said, "Get out here and let's get this over with."

The bedroom door opened wider and Doyle could see Skeeter standing in the darkness. Suddenly, he saw Skeeter bring up the rifle and aim. Doyle dove to the end of the couch, the bullet barely missing him. His Sig was out of reach, but he had his back-up piece, the .38, in its holster behind him. He pulled it out just as Skeeter moved out of the bedroom aiming the rifle. Doyle brought the .38 up and fired, hitting Skeeter in the thigh. Skeeter spun and dropped the rifle. Doyle ran to him lying on the floor, kicking the rifle away.

Doyle grabbed Skeeter by the wrist and dragged him to the end of the couch where the bomb was attached. In the process of dragging him, he tripped the wire, causing the box to make a loud ticking noise. Doyle pulled a zip-cuff and strapped Skeeter's left wrist to the arm of the couch, next to the bomb.

"Well, it seems I accidently set your bomb in motion. But, since you built it, you can disarm it, right?"

Skeeter was in pain and said nothing. Doyle looked to the box and saw the timer counting down. There was less than two minutes. "Well, I can't take the bomb out since you chained it to the couch, I can't do anything about the bomb, so I'm getting out of here. You better get to work on disarming it. It's your only chance to survive, then I'll see you in jail."

Doyle move to the door after recovering his Sig from the couch. "Sorry if I don't hang around, but you remember me as a coward, so keep that image in your worthless head. Say hi to all your victims." Doyle started to go out as Skeeter was screaming for him to come back.

"Doyle! I can't disarm this thing with one hand. You bastard!" Skeeter screamed.

"Then you better move fast, it's your only chance," Doyle shouted over his shoulder as he hurried out of the cabin.

Doyle was walking down the drive to his car and he saw Oscar standing in the road.

"Where's Skeeter?" Oscar asked.

"Last I saw, he was hanging around to disarm the bomb." Doyle turned, looking back.

Suddenly, there was a tremendous explosion and the front of the cabin blew outward. Doyle felt a twinge of regret about his cabin, but he couldn't save it. Skeeter saw to that.

"Guess he couldn't disarm in time," Oscar said. "Too bad, he had such a nice plan for you."

"How's Amber?"

"Still out. Shall I see if I can wake her?"

"No, let her rest. I'm calling the fire department and Mike. Now that we are free from Skeeter, we can relax." Doyle pulled his cell phone and placed the calls.

An hour later, the fire was out as the firemen were hosing down the rest of the building. The cabin was pretty much destroyed, much to Doyle's regret. He definitely wouldn't forget Skeeter as Skeeter had promised.

Amber was now up and standing next to Doyle. "I think we need to see a little less of each other. You're too dangerous for my health."

Doyle laughed, "I live a busy life, but we can visit each other once in a while, if that's all right?"

"That will work, once in a while." She kissed his cheek and went back to Doyle's car to sit.

Mike came up and said, "If Skeeter was in there, Elwood is going to have fits finding his body parts. So you left him to disarm the bomb?"

"That's what happened. The bomb was attached to my couch so I couldn't get it out of the cabin. I told Skeeter to see if he could shut it off. I guess he couldn't. Poor bastard," Doyle said with a smirk.

"Good thing you left him alone to do it, or we'd be picking up pieces of you, too."

"I'm not crazy. I'll run when the occasion merits it. I remember that saying 'He who fights and runs away, lives to fight another day.' It fits this situation."

"I'll put that in my report," Mike said with a smile.

*

195

Chapter 31

Doyle dropped Amber off at her apartment and they said their goodbyes at her door. "I'll call when I'm in town, if you feel up to it, no promises."

"Sounds good. Thank you, Art, it's been an interesting week. I've jumped out of a moving vehicle, was shot at, been knocked out and came close to being blown up by a bomb. That's something not all woman can say."

"No, it isn't, and you've been very brave through it all. I'll see you again." He gave her a kiss, then turned away and went to his car. Oscar was sitting quietly. "So, nothing to say?" he asked Oscar.

"Nope, I was just going over the night in my head. You left him there, didn't you?"

"It was his choice, to disarm the bomb or die. I guess we'll never know. When I left him, I wasn't thinking so much about Skeeter's life, I was thinking about the victims he murdered. And about saving my own life. That bomb was set to go off in less than two minutes and there was no time to hang around the cabin. I gave Skeeter the option to disarm it. He evidently either couldn't, or he just wanted to die."

"I'm not passing judgment. I would have strapped the damn bomb to him and set him loose. He was a worthless piece of crap. The world is a far better place today without him in it. So, are we back in business of chasing cheating spouses again?"

"Looks that way. Mike said there was nothing for us to do here, I explained everything to him and I'll call the insurance company in the morning. My poor cabin, I had so many memories there."

"You'll probably get a nice new cabin built. Just make sure the kitchen is well stocked," Oscar said with a grin.

"Just like you to think about food. I may want a real kitchen, separate from the rest of the cabin. I may have them build a small house instead of a cabin. A place I can retire to in ten years or so. I'll be in my sixties then and I can relax by the lake."

They drove back to Doyle's Detroit apartment and Oscar took his car home. Doyle went in and headed straight for the shower. He relaxed and put on the soft music station, then he sat with a beer in hand and went over the past few days in his head. He wasn't really happy with the way he left Skeeter, but justice was served, and his conscience was clear. He was now feeling very tired and fell asleep on the couch.

The next morning, Marge was back at her desk. Doyle called her the night before and said it was all right to come in. She was happy to be back and got the office back in order. She had brought in a large potted plant that she set in the front window, she said to make the room look nice. Doyle moved her desk closer to the door so she could talk to prospective clients first before she turned them over to him or Oscar. She turned on her radio and had it set to a nice classic music station. The music was relaxing to hear in the big room.

Oscar was now sitting next to her desk telling her the sordid tale of murder and mayhem they just went through.

Doyle sat at his desk smiling as Oscar went through the motions of telling the story. It was nice not to have the partition walls, so he could see out the front window and watch Marge and Oscar. He was watching the traffic moving slowly out front when he saw three men coming to his front door. He waited as they entered. Oscar got up and went over to his desk.

Marge smiled and asked what they wanted. There were two very big men in suits, the third man was a bit smaller. Suddenly, Doyle recognized the smaller man. It was the mayor of Detroit. Doyle cringed, wondering what he wanted. Was he coming to complain about Doyle shooting him?

Marge looked over to Doyle as he stood, coming to the men. "Mr. Mayor, what brings you here?"

"Doyle, I've had some time to think about what you did, and my wife said I was acting like an ass and being petty. She said you saved my butt and I should have been grateful. Looking back, I am very grateful. I just wanted to apologize for the way I acted. I was under a lot of stress from the kidnapping and you shooting Crazy Joe just shook me up. Not to mention hitting me on the side of the head with that bullet that took out Joe. It's healing well and there will be a slight scar, so I'll remember my ordeal. Doyle, I hope you can accept my apology?"

"Mr. Mayor, it was a pleasure to have saved your life. Now you have to save Detroit."

"I'm working on it. If there's anything you ever need, let me know and I'll see what I can do. Maybe you'll come back to the PD, maybe I could promote you to Captain?"

Doyle thought of Cadeem and smiled. "I'll think about it. But I'm happy with less stress here."

"Well, keep my offer in mind. I checked on you and you were an exemplary detective."

"Thank you, sir."

The mayor signaled to his two men, who Doyle figured were his bodyguards, and they went out. Oscar came over and stood smiling. "What's on your devious little mind?" Doyle asked.

"Captain Doyle, it has a nice ring," Oscar said.

"No thank you, too much work at a desk. I like working the field better. Now we need to get some clients in to get our business rolling again."

Marge came over and took a black knit scarf out of a paper bag and put it around Doyle's neck. "I made it for you. I have one for Oscar, too. Can't have you boys getting chilled this winter."

"And it's coming fast now. Thank you, Marge, it's good to have you back," Doyle said and gave her a kiss on the cheek.

"Great to be back. I loved staying with my sister, but she drove me crazy the last couple days. Good to be back in my own home, too." She smiled and went over to her desk.

Doyle took the scarf and put it on his desk. The front door opened and in came a man dressed very well in an expensive looking suit. He went to Marge and said, "I need to hire a private investigator. My art gallery is being pilfered."

Doyle looked at Oscar and said, "We're back in business."

*

THE END

Visit with Doyle, Oscar and Marge in their next adventure, "Doyle's Quest" Here's a preview.

Chapter 1

Marge smiled at the well-dressed man standing before her desk. "I am curator for the Wittington Art Gallery on Woodward and I think someone is stealing our pieces and substituting very clever forgeries. I need a private investigator to find the culprit."

Marge looked to Doyle who was sitting at his desk. He nodded to her and said, "Send him to me."

Oscar went back to his desk, after talking with Doyle about building up business. Marge pointed and said for the man to go to Doyle. He walked the short distance to the desk and stood waiting. Doyle got up from his chair and said, "Please have a seat." He pointed to his client chair and the man went around to sit. Doyle sat and asked, "Now why do you think someone is stealing from your gallery?"

"I know it's going on. I've had various articles examined and the consensus is, they are fakes. The originals are missing."

"When did you first realize that this was happening?"

"About a week ago. One of our valuable statues was knocked off its pedestal and broke. I saw that the interior of the statue was made of plaster. This statue was not supposed to be plaster, it was supposed to be granite. There was even a weight inside to make the thing heavy, like granite."

"So, you've had more art items examined?" Doyle asked.

"I did, and out of the ten I took in to be checked, four were fakes. The value of the art work in question was in the thousands of dollars."

"What's your take on how this could happen?"

Doyle's Justice

"I'm not paid to investigate; I'm curator of the gallery. This is why I'm here to hire you."

His statement didn't make it any easier to get an idea of what could have happened. "Of course, that's my job. But it would help to get an idea of where I can start. Do you suspect your employees? Or do you think this could be an outside job? You must have an opinion."

The man hesitated, then said, "I think it was an inside job, as the police say. One of the employees must be behind this. I can't just fire all our people to stop one thief, so I need your help."

"Well, I'll need to stop by and check out your set-up to get a feel for how the articles could be removed and replaced," Doyle said. "May I have access to the entire building, the gallery and the back areas? I presume you have a shipping dock and storage?"

"Yes, we do, and I'll see you have access to all areas. I have the board of directors to answer to, so I need to get this handled quickly and discretely."

"I am the epitome of discrete investigators," Doyle said, and noticed that Oscar was holding in a laugh.

"Very well. Come to my office tomorrow morning and I'll give you a tour of the facility. Many of our acquisitions are on loan from friendly countries. It would be very bad if they found their treasures were being pilfered."

"I understand. I'll meet with you in the morning."

"I hate to bring it up, but what about your fees?"

"We charge $200 a day while on the job, five percent recovery fee, and expenses, which we will provide receipts for."

"That sounds reasonable. Considering the cost of our missing articles, you should do well with your recovery fee. I'll see you then." He stood and held out his hand. Doyle took it and they said their goodbyes. On his way to the door, the man nodded to Marge and left the building.

Oscar came rushing over. "Art gallery, and your name is Art, it's karma. Are you going to get one of those hats like Indiana Jones wears?"

"Why would I do that?" Doyle asked.

"Well, you're going to hunt for missing artifacts like Jones did. So you'll need a hat."

"I don't wear hats, other than an occasional baseball cap. And, I'm not Indiana Jones, so don't start spreading that around." Doyle tried not to smile, but he did. "I always liked Jones, maybe I'll see if I can find that hat."

Marge came over. "I know just the place where they have those hats. It a little shop called Harry the Hatter. My Max used to go there to get his hats. Max looked so good in a hat. I'll see if they still carry the Indiana Jones hats."

Doyle started laughing, "I think I'd look silly, but just take a look and see. I'm not saying I would wear one, but…"

Marge's phone rang and she went back to her desk, sat and answered. "Doyle and Drew investigations," she said. Doyle decided to give Oscar some credit in the name of the firm. Doyle and Drew had a nice ring to it. "May I help you?" She listened then said, "Hold one minute." She clicked the hold button and turned to Oscar. "You have a Mr. Greenstreet calling about his wife. The one you followed the other day."

"Ah, yes, the wife cheating with his best friend. I'll take the call." Oscar went back to his desk and picked up the phone.

Doyle went to Marge's desk and sat. "Do you think I would look good in one of those Indy hats?"

"You have a well chiseled face, rugged and bold. I think you'd look great."

"I know you're just blowing smoke up my shorts, but thanks. Maybe I'll take a look at them."

"Good, I'll write down the directions to Harry the Hatter. He's been in business for over sixty years. He makes hats for many famous people, too."

"Okay, sounds good," Doyle said as Oscar came over. "You look serious, what's up?"

"That was my client for the cheating wife I followed yesterday. Seems she was murdered last night and he wants me to provide the police with everything I had while I was following her."

"That's privileged, but if he's okay with sharing it, then get it all ready to go. Did he ask if we could investigate the murder?"

"He said the police are investigating, which they should be. I mentioned that an independent investigation may help his case, since he is under suspicion for the murder. He said he'd let us know."

"Good. We just got back from finding a serial killer for no pay, now maybe we'll have some income," Doyle said and looked at Marge. "I'd like to pay you better than I have. You deserve it."

"Oh goodness, I'm not worrying about it, just gas money and pay for the coffee, I'm happy," she said with a smile.

"Yeah, we'll work on it. If this gallery has thousands of dollars in articles stolen, we should get a hefty recovery fee. First I have to find out who the thief is, and then recover the stolen goods."

"You may have to travel to Egypt to recover the items. An Indy hat would shade you nicely."

"I doubt I'll have to go further than the streets of Detroit to find the items," Doyle said, then continued, "Marge, order a large pizza with everything from Cloverleaf Pizza and have it delivered. I think we have enough in petty cash to cover it."

"Yes, we do for one pizza, then petty cash is tapped out."

"I'll have to withdraw a little money from the bank to bolster up the fund."

Marge called to order the pizza, Oscar went to get his files on the murdered wife together, and Doyle stood looking in the mirror on the back wall wondering how he'd look in a hat.

About an hour later, they had their fill of pizza and were sitting around talking. "I called the insurance company about rebuilding my cabin since

Skeeter blew it up. They said they're sending an agent to discuss the policy I have. I've kept up the payments, so I'm not worried. I just hope they don't give me a hard time. The insurance agent is supposed to be here after noon."

"Arthur, it is after noon," Marge said, just as the front door opened. In came a woman, around her late thirties, well dressed in a skirt showing nice legs, suit jacket, and carrying a valise. She was very attractive and had shoulder length auburn hair. "I think your insurance agent is here," Marge said, getting up and going to the woman.

"I think your next girlfriend just came in," Oscar grinned and went back to his desk.

Doyle didn't give Marge much of a chance to talk to the woman, he was right there next to them. "Arthur, this lady is from your insurance company. I'll let you two get acquainted." Marge went to her desk and picked up her knitting.

"I'm Julia Drake, from American Life and Casualty, and I'm here about your cabin."

"Pleasure to meet you Julia, may I call you Julia? You can call me Art. Please, come and sit at my desk." He led her there and pulled the client chair closer to his chair. She sat and so did he. They were closely facing each other. She looked a little uncomfortable, so Doyle pushed his chair back a little.

"So, what do you need to know? My cabin was blown up by a crazed serial killer and it's a wreck. I've had the cabin for almost twenty years, since just before I went into the FBI. I was in a terrorist tactical team." Doyle was starting to babble. He stopped talking and asked her to proceed.

"Thank you. I haven't been to the site of the destruction yet, to evaluate, so I can't say what will need to be done to fix your building."

"Oh, it can't be fixed. It's burnt out pretty good. It'll have to be razed and a new building put up. I'd be more than happy to drive you to the property so you can see it," he said, hoping she would go with him.

"That's all right, I'll have my boyfriend drive me up."

Doyle could hear Oscar snickering.

*

Continued in the book…

Jim Richards series books by Bob Moats

(In series order)
Classmate Murders
Vegas Showgirl Murders
Dominatrix Murders
Mistress Murders
Bridezilla Murders
Magic Murders
Strip Club Murders
Made-for-TV Murders
Mystery Cruise Murders
Talk Show Murders
Sin City Murders
Black Widow Murders
Vegas Vigilante Murders
Area 51 Murders
Mortuary Murders
Hypnotic Murders
Sunshine State Murders
Blue Suede Murders
Honky Tonk Murders
Dark Carnival Murders
Lipstick Murders
Pasta Murders
Talent Show Murders
Shyster Murders
Campground Murders
Network Murders
Reunion Murders
Big Apple Murders
Kennel Murders
Trick or Treat Murders
Santa Murders
Wiseguy Murders

For a preview or to purchase a book, go to
http://murdernovels.com

What a few people are saying about the Jim Richards Murder Novels by Bob Moats

Mr. Moats, I just got your novel "Classmate Murders" and have to let you know, I read it in one evening. That is the first book I have ever done that with. That was the most enjoyable book I have ever read. I just started reading e-books, and reading again, after getting my wife a Kindle. This book was my 12th, and the best. I just got Las Vegas Showgirls to (read) tomorrow evening. I look forward to reading many of your books in this series. I have been searching for an author and books that were fun, entertaining reads. Your books are just the ticket.

Regards, A new fan, Bill from South Carolina

****

Hi Bob, I just had to write you... Last week I purchased a Nook Soft Touch e-reader. I was downloading free e-books and downloaded "Classmate Murders" from Barnes & Noble. I read it that night and enjoyed it so much that I went to search for the next one (as listed at end of the book). Read it and searched again. After reading the second one, I did a search from my e-reader for you and bought ALL of the books. So in the last week I have read all of the Jim Richards books. Finished the last one early this morning. I only read at night 10-6 when my neighbor is asleep. As I read the books I sometimes laughed and sometimes cried. I could relate to Jim as we are both in the 60s. I liked how "Jim" refers to previous murders in each book. That is great for anyone who has not read the books in order and also as fast as I did. Anyway, I just had to write and tell you how much I enjoyed the books.

Nancie S.

****

Another very nice comment submitted through my website from Micki P.:

"I recently was given a kindle for my 60th birthday. The first book I downloaded was the Classmate Murders and have now read every one of the them. Today I started on the Fatal Rejection series. Thank you for the wonderful ride with Jim and Penny and all the rest of the troop. I have laughed and giggled thru the stories, my poor family gave me the strangest looks! Now I really want a little Yorkie!! Fatal Rejection so far is another great read! I will be looking out for more of Jim Richards and since you are my #1 Author, anything of yours I can find."

Thank you for purchasing this book. I hope you enjoy it as much as I enjoyed writing it for my faithful readers. If you liked the book please feel free to write an honest review on the product page where you got this book from. I'd appreciate it. Please feel free to email me to tell me what you thought about my stories. I love hearing from the readers. I can be reached at murdernovels@bobmoats.com thanks again!